Tales from an Allotment Site

by

Belle France

Contents

Sugar - The Day Before

The fire brigade recovery truck left, closely followed by the fire engine and the mud-bespattered ambulance. Sugar was in the back with his nether regions wrapped up in silver foil and he still hadn't come round.

6 am isn't as early as it used to be; gone are the days when I needed to be woken by an alarm clock at 7.30 am. Nowadays, I lie there awake, checking the clock every few minutes waiting for a respectable time to get up. I now class 6 am as a respectable time. It was a lovely sunny but cold morning when I got to the allotment. I had to watch my footing—it had been rainy the past few days which made the allotment paths boggy. Last night had been clear and bright with an early morning frost but promised to be a lovely sunny spring day. No one was here. I crossed over to the other side of the path as I passed John Farthing's gate.

It's a lovely time of the day, peaceful and quiet. I enjoy the walk through the quiet paths with well-kept allotments either side. I like nosing at what the other plot holders are growing and getting ideas for next year. Often you catch site of the foxes; they look at me with surprise on their faces. We have every

1

type of bird visit us, from robins to buzzards; they are all lovely but they are the main competitors for the crops, along with
the slugs and various types of insects. When I first started
growing, I was so excited that I could take a seed, plant it, nur-
ture it, love it until it grew into a seedling, then I would spend
hours of back-breaking work planting, watering, feeding, ensuring they were just the right width apart. Keeping the areas
weed free, at the end of the day, I would stand at my rickety
wooden garden gate (found in a skip), looking back to admire
my crops with such pride, trying to estimate when I could take
one of my lovely cabbages home ready to eat. On my return
the next day, all I had was rows of pencils, all my lovely cabbages decimated overnight by the birds.

We (the eight committee members) had set aside part of one
corner plot to collect scrap metal found around the site and
leave it there until it was a decent amount. Then we would get
the metal man in to collect all the metal and weigh it in and go
halves on the amount he gets. We saved this money up and after about eighteen months we had saved up enough to buy a
big trailer. We continued to collect metal but now weighed it
in ourselves, keeping all the money to fund work that needed
doing on site. A couple of the committee members would load
the metal and take it all down to Hawkins the scrap man and

cash it in. The trailer was also handy for if he found sheds or greenhouses people didn't want anymore. We picked them up, brought them on the site and sold them on to plot holders, charging them £25 for the shed and £25 for the greenhouse, again all the money going to the society for works around site. We raised money for various improvements: CCTV, new hedgerows and renewing the paths. Our next purchase would be a big shed to store rotavators and gardening equipment in. The metal was a decent amount—it threw a shadow over the path I walked down, changing my walk from a pleasant stroll along the paths to a walk through a scrapyard as it grew daily. Quite soon there would be a working party and a trip to Hawkins to weigh it in as the price of metal was quite high.

Vandalism and theft are blights to an allotmenteer. It is much cheaper to visit the allotments to get fresh veg than walk down the road to Asda, and to add a bit of excitement you can throw stones at the greenhouses and see how much glass you can break. Or ransack sheds, breaking the door down first, or just have a good burn. Last year, they took all the potatoes that covered one side of Corner George's plot and stripped the courgette plants from another. Every plum from Peter's two trees had been taken; they must have come in with a car or van—either very late or very early as they are never seen—

which is why the society decided to use our reserve funds to put CCTV cameras on each of the gates, causing much annoyance to a certain group of plot holders claiming their privacy has been invaded.

It was the norm that as soon as I got to my shed I put the kettle on to make a cup of tea, then spent the first hour or two just pottering and enjoying the solitude before the other folk arrived. That morning, as usual, I put the kettle on, and whilst it was boiling I went on an early morning inspection of my plot to see what damage the weather, vandals, birds and slugs had done overnight.

As I walked down the wet and wobbly path to my plot, out of the corner of my eye I caught a ray of sunshine bouncing off a large floral lump on top of the shed next to mine. I had to strain my eyes from the sun to try to work out what it was. Eventually, I got close enough to Danny's shed, with its "roof garden" as he calls it, to inspect the lump: it had twig-like legs clad in knee-length Hawaiian shorts. It was Sugar!

He was always wearing shorts, whatever the weather; he said he had "shummer and winzer" shorts. They all looked the same to me. I shouted 'morning' but no answer. After several more 'mornings' and a few 'hellos' I went over to Danny's shed and tried again in the desperate hope that he would hear me, but with no luck. I walked round the back of the shed. I had never ventured round the back before but possibly, subconsciously, I was hoping to find a staircase or an escalator. He had a glass lean-to greenhouse, about two feet deep and the length of the shed. I had never seen it before. It was full of what looked like large flowerless lupins.

Against my better judgement, I got Danny's old rickety wooden ladder which was lying on the ground and leaned it on his equally rickety shed and bravely climbed up. I shook Sugar. Nothing. I noticed that Dirty Gertie the scarecrow and the two gnomes which were Danny's pride and joy had suffered. The fishing gnome was shoved headfirst into the soil and the peeing gnome was wearing a cider can over his privates. Sugar lay face up with his arm around Gertie the scarecrow. He was gripping another empty can of cider, an Asda bag full of empty cans next to him. The ladder started to move and a wave of panic came over me.

My mum laid people out: that is to say, when someone died in our street they came for my mum as she could 'lay people out'. These days that means they'll knock you out, but not back then. I was about seven when Mrs Foster next door died suddenly and my mum was asked by her distraught husband to 'lay her out'. I asked her what 'laying out' was and she explained. I was horrified at how she could touch a dead body then make my tea. 'How did you know that they were really, really dead? They might have just been having a good sleep or fainted?' I asked. Mum gave me a variety of reasons including the doctor had written a death certificate but added, 'You can always tell 'cos they go the colour of boiled shite.'

Sugar was the colour of boiled shite. I looked down at his loud floral shorts and realised he was wringing wet and freezing cold and there was a smell of urine. I could hear the kettle in my shed starting to whistle. The ladder decided to move again, the panic wave stepped up a notch. I kept still for a minute and hoped the ladder would too. Gingerly, I tried to release his hand from the can. I don't know why I did it, it wouldn't make any difference to the situation, nonetheless, I tried a few times—it was either frozen or he just wasn't letting go. I tried to move Dirty Gertie, the name Danny had given the scarecrow as the tartan kilt she wore lifted when the wind caught it, showing her knickers. He and the other blokes thought this was hilarious. Sugar had a firm grip on Gertie and cuddled her next to his head. The kettle was in full throttle and out of the corner

6

of my eye I could see the steam bellowing out from my shed. The ladder moved again as I fumbled around trying to find Sugar's pulse, wishing I had taken the opportunity to learn first aid.

I stretched over and tried his wrist, then stretched further to try and reach his neck but gave up when the ladder started to move. I heard that you can check a pulse on the top inner side of the thigh. No way was I putting my hand up his Hawaiians. The panic wave started moving at speed up and down my body, making me tremble all over. My nerves were stretched and I could feel a tightening in my chest. I kept trying to focus on helping Sugar. Again I tried waking him up, but realised he was more in a coma than asleep. I thought of getting on the roof to try and move him. Images flew through my mind of Danny building this shed with its "roof garden" and the amount of soil and water that formed the roof, not to mention the ladder with a mind of its own. No one was around to help me try and move Sugar and he was freezing. There was still frost on his shorts so I decided to find something to cover him with then call an ambulance. I dismounted the ladder, and when I finally got back to my shed shaking with fright, the kettle had boiled dry and the red plastic handle, whistle and knob had melted into a bubbling red cowpat of plastic running down the now black kettle. I turned the camp stove off and found my phone. I tried to tap in 999 but I was freezing and shaking, so I sat down and tried to gather myself together. The pain in my chest started to ease. I needed to hurry but each time I tried the pain increased. I felt I was dilly-dallying over getting help but I needed to calm myself to ease it.

By the time I got to the allotment, it was covered in brambles. With the old shed full of rubbish, my first job was to clean it out. After my six-year-old granddaughter's first visit, she saved up her pocket money and went to her local charity shop and bought me shed-warming presents: one pair of net curtains to make it homely, a Snow White oval mirror, and a picture with a price tag of £2.50 which she got for 50p as that is all she had left. The lady serving simply crossed out the £2 and said it had supposed to be reduced yesterday and gave her the old nicotine-stained oil painting of a seaside scene—I could just make the signature out as *A. Meluille*. The stained painting, the now not-so-white oval mirror and the curtains, which the mice were slowly eating their way through, would always bring happy memories flooding back of Megan, my lovely grand-daughter, whenever I looked at them. I longed to see her but she was with my daughter Emma and husband Alan who went to live in Queensland, Australia for just two years. That was four years ago and there was no sign of them coming back. I looked up at the mirror; the white wrinkly face looking back at me was the same colour as Sugar: boiled shite.

I eventually managed to ring the ambulance. I then I found a few metres of greyish-white fleece used to keep the seedlings warmer in spring. I braved the ladder again and did my best to wrap Sugar up head to toe in the fleece. I tried to remove Gertie again but then thought the better of it. After all, he had a vice-like grip on her and she was probably the only female company he had had. I climbed down the ladder, opened the site gate and waited for the ambulance. The pain had now eased and I looked a better colour.

We nicknamed him "Sugar" as he was always drinking cider. *Scrumpy Jack* was his "cider of choice" as they say; he drank it all day and every day. Initially, we called him Scrumpy Jack, but as the economy worsened he had to lower his standards and now drinks whatever cider is on special at the local supermarket. Forcing us to give him a more generic name, Danny renamed him Sugar because as he drunkenly wobbled by the plots, he reminded him of Freddie Frinton, an old comedian who did a great act of a drunk with a broken cigarette in his mouth; he had a drunken sideways walk with one hand ahead of him and one behind singing Ruby Murray's *Sugar in the Morning*. Every time Sugar walks by it is hard to resist breaking into a chorus of *Sugar in the morning, sugar in the evening, sugar at super time*, so he was renamed Sugar.

It is common practice on the allotment to give pen names to plot holders. A small group of us had renamed nearly all the plot holders around us. What started out as a bit of fun had now become an accepted way of identifying people. Obviously *I* have a name—I am one half of the Marigold Girls, Kitty being the other half, so named as we garden in "Marigolds" to save our hands.

Sugar has been found drunk all over the site, not just drunk but *really, really* drunk—the kind that is completely incoherent—and as he gets more drunk he tends to walk sideways with his right arm leading the way and his left held back as though it doesn't want to be involved and is pulling to go in another direction (just like Freddie Frinton, only in Hawaiian shorts).

He has been found lying in veg patches, against hedges where he has just been stumbling along, passed out and fallen sideways into the hedge. Once he passed out at the big double gates as he was trying to unlock them to get out. It must have proven too difficult in his state: the security CCTV camera showed him just slip forward onto the gate and slide down until he was in a sitting position and passed out. As he slipped down, the back of his shorts caught on the gate bar, pulling the legs of his floral shorts tight round his crotch; although fat in body, he has long stick-thin legs and with his old green wellies sticking out, he looked like Bill and Ben from the 1960s. No one could get in or out until they managed to wake him up. We laughed about it as it was funny, but at the same time not. Another time, George, that is "Corner George" as he has a corner plot, arrived early to find just a pair of legs sticking out of his laurel hedge. After further inspection, he assisted Sugar out of the hedge and watched him wobble down the lane doing his Freddie Frinton walk with his Asda bag full of empty cider cans, which he keeps in his bin until the metal man comes around again and then trades them in.

On the plot next to me is Danny who has put a "roof garden" on his shed. It has about two tons of soil on it, is ten inches deep, and it slopes downwards towards the path in order that people passing by can enjoy the wild flower garden experience. Danny went to great lengths to explain to me how it was built, where he got the idea from; as his pièce de résistance, he threw a packet of wild flower seeds on top and watered it religiously every day until the grass and the flowers grew. He keeps repeating in his Yorkshire accent that he 'Am rit proud of it' but it's a mess—the only things that do stand on it are the local animals: feral tom cats, foxes, birds and even a polecat. I have seen them on many a morning, although seeing isn't the only way we know they have been on the roof; their toilet and the foxes' urine smell terrible when combined with the tom cats. If that isn't bad enough, Danny smokes very strange smelling cigarettes and the smell seems to seep through the roof adding to the mix of aromas.

When you enter his shed (should you be brave or foolhardy enough) the strange smelling cigarettes seem to hang in the air and, after just a few minutes, you begin to feel light headed. This is probably to ease the feeling of being in imminent danger of a collapsing roof.

He put a lot of effort into building it, reinforcing the sides to take the weight of the roof—but left out the middle supports as they would be in his way and not really needed—, then covering it in some sort of waterproof membrane to stop water going through, followed by a layer of wire mesh to keep the soil in place. He then carried buckets and buckets of soil up on a rickety old ladder, spreading it over the roof.

He got the design idea after visiting his native home, Kingston, Jamaica, then researching on the internet, and insists it is perfectly safe. Two weeks later, it was showing green stubble, which was ugly in itself; now it has long grass with dandelions sticking out. As if that wasn't bad enough, he then placed two gnomes on it, one fishing and one peeing, then stuck the scarecrow wearing a tartan skirt in one corner. No expense gone to, they were all from the pound shop. It's awful but he is so proud of it, so we all say how good it is and how clever he is but worry every time he is in there and it starts to rain, just waiting for it to collapse under the weight—and no amount of fig biscuits and tea will get me in there. I am convinced it is going to collapse and I don't intend to be in there when it does.

Yesterday was a lovely sunny early spring day with a very clear, starry night. Sugar must have been on the cider all day again and decided to take a nap on Danny's roof garden, attempting to climb up, stepping onto the metal drum next to the shed which is used to collect the rain water. It's never full as most rain is sitting on the roof garden waiting for the shed to be full of "the old" before collapsing on them. Sugar mustn't have noticed that the plastic lid of the drum had decayed and was split down the middle. In an effort to get on the roof, he must have climbed on the lid then sunk slowly down into the drum up to his waist in water. How he extracted himself from this I don't know, but when I got here the water drum was over on its side and all the water drained down the path. His wet shoes and shorts had turned to ice now. Somehow, he must have climbed onto the roof, lain down and gone to sleep or passed out. I was thankful he somehow extracted himself from the drum; had he passed out in the drum, the sight greeting me this morning could have been a human ice lolly.

After a very clear night, we had a frost. Only a light one but when you're wringing wet up to and past your nether regions it can't be good. He was freezing cold and his clothes were wet from the waist down and the frost had turned them crunchy to the touch. Plus I think he had added to the urine smell.

After ten minutes, the ambulance drove slowly down our narrow lane. There is only one way in and out as the other end of our lane has a six-foot hedge. The male and female crew got out of the ambulance and asked me where the patient was, so I pointed to the shed. They looked very smart in their uniforms. I was very impressed and admired their professionalism as I started to explain what had happened.

The ambulance crew busied themselves getting packs and machinery from the ambulance. By the time they started up the path, the warmth of the sun on Danny's roof garden created a damp haze over the roof. Birds were circling and squawking in the air above, the fleece resembled a greyish-white shroud; we could see Dirty Gertie's head sticking out next to his face. It looked like a ritual had taken place, an offering to the gods. I heard a voice whispering, 'Jeesis.' Two other plot holders, Pretty Penny and Fat Mick, had now arrived and stood open-mouthed at the sight. The ambulance lady gasped and the male crew member just stared, aghast.

I managed to explain what had happened as the ambulance crew regained their composure. They walked up my path, then ran up the rickety ladder and tried to wake him. When that didn't work they tried to move him. Sugar is about five foot ten and well overweight, so the ambulance crew—a slightly built male and his female colleague—stood no chance of moving him. When they asked for volunteers to get on the roof garden to assist them to get him down, they were met with silence. I explained the construction of the roof and that's when they decided to wrap Sugar up in silver foil, climbed down and called for the fire brigade. Fifteen minutes later, the fire crew arrived and backed down the narrow path. This was to ensure they could leave quickly if they got a real "shout".

It took four firefighters to get him off the roof and into the ambulance. Gertie had fallen onto the path and the officer in charge picked her up and gave her to me. The female of the crew climbed into the ambulance and began checking Sugar over while the male asked for information on him. I had seen him more or less daily for the past six years and I neglected to say that I had laughed and taken the mickey out of him along with everyone else, but I knew nothing. Except that his real name was Jack, he lost his mum a couple of years ago, that he was very friendly with Irish Pat, a war veteran, but he too had died a couple of years ago, that he lived in a flat close by, and that he drank far too much. They should call the site secretary, John Farthing, for further information.

The lanes on our site are very narrow and not made for cars let alone ambulances, and definitely not large fire engines. This site is one of the oldest in England; the paths were designed for walking on or wheelbarrows. Or if you were well off, a bike at best, but not motorised vehicles. The winter had been one of the wettest on record and many of the plots were waterlogged. Many allotmenteers dug a foot-wide trench down one side of their plot to drain the water away onto the paths. We have designated car parks around the site as driving down these little lanes, especially when wet, often means you get bogged down—but this was an emergency.

The firefighters had done their job and were a very jovial team as they swaggered down the path towards the fire engine. 'An easy start to our shift' as one of them put it. They spoke to the ambulance crew again and smiled happily as they climbed into the fire engine to leave. They turned the engine on and it roared into action, but as they revved the back wheels of the engine span round and sank into the mud-sodden path which had been made a lot wetter by the overturned water drum and the warming sun melting the morning frost. They revved again and again. I was in my shed dealing with the red mass that once was my kettle when I heard shouting from the ambulance crew and roars of laughter from the watching people that had now gathered.

The revving from the back wheels of the fire engine had sprayed mud into the back of the open ambulance. Sugar and the crew were covered in mud. The crew swore loudly at the firefighters and the back doors of the ambulance closed with a bang. The more they revved the more stuck they became and the more mud they sprayed up the back of the now closed ambulance door and the more the fire fighters swore. They were stuck fast and it was getting worse. The jovial group of firefighters had resorted to a seething mass of swear words as they tried to rock, push and put bricks under wheels until, embarrassingly, they had to send for reinforcements. Intermittently, the back door of the ambulance would open a few inches and a voice would ask for an update, that they needed to get Sugar to hospital. The reply was littered with muttered swear words and general abuse aimed at anyone, including the ambulance crew.

I took the British fail-safe position and made tea. I steeled myself to enter Danny's shed to borrow his kettle and made cups of tea while the firefighters waited for the recovery vehicle. The ambulance crew remained with Sugar in the ambulance; they were very concerned as he had at the very least hypothermia and frostbite in one of his fingers and in his nether regions.

The mood of the firefighters was made worse when they got a "real" shout and had to pass it on to another fire crew: they couldn't attend and had to explain why. It was at that point that I think they began to seek revenge and became interested in Danny's roof garden and its construction. They asked ques-

18

tions about it: what were Danny's qualifications in building, how much soil was on top? And whilst I boiled the borrowed kettle, they went to have a look inside.

After about thirty minutes, a huge truck arrived and I mean HUGE. It was like a real Tonka Truck; everything around it looked minuscule and it was squashing all the hedges or anything else that got in its way. It too backed down the lane and attached a thick chain and hook to the fire engine before trying to pull it out. The noise was deafening as the fire engine revved again and again. The Tonka Truck was dragging and pulling at the engine. At first, I thought it wouldn't move it, as the more it pulled the more soil it sprayed up the ambulance as the engine tried to move forward. The recovery truck eventually moved it, jerking it forward with a bump, then the engine started to move forward under its own steam, bouncing from side to side and leaving deep potholes in the path.

The ambulance was now caked in mud, and when both of the fire vehicles were safely away, the male member got out to clean the mud off the back doors and the side mirrors before setting off. The firefighters were now safely away and out of earshot as he shouted abuse after them.

Danny had arrived as the engines were leaving. He stood open-mouthed, looking around at the mud-covered ambulance, the fire engine and the recovery vehicles. I walked down the path with Dirty Gertie and knocked at the ambulance door. The male crew member opened the ambulance door and I gave him Dirty Gertie. I asked him to give her to Sugar, as he seemed to like her, and asked for an update. I felt dreadful. Danny was still bemused, looking from person to person and at the state of the path, then staring into the back of the ambulance.

Sugar was lying on the bed, still out with the young uniformed female who was gently talking to him whilst carefully wrapping his "block and tackle" (as he later called it) in silver foil. Danny was, to say the least, mystified, bewildered and envious. The small crowd of plot holders stood there, including Pretty Penny, Fat Mick and Danny—all open-mouthed.

The ambulance left very carefully, bouncing up and down and from side to side—it looked like a toy ambulance. We could hear banging and clattering from things falling about inside. This was mixed with extremely bad language as it bounced down in the holes the Tonka Truck had made. Eventually, it levelled out and off they went down the lane to take Sugar to hospital.

20

The sun was getting warmer. The chest pains had completely gone. I made a promise to myself to see the doctor. I made another cup of tea, set the table up and regaled Danny, Pretty Penny and Fat Mick of the tale to date. After the amusement, the moans began: what about the mess they had left the lane in, it would gather water, get icy, be dangerous, someone should tell the site secretary and complain to the council, 'this will all come out of our rates, you know, it's *our* money being wasted here'. Pretty Penny went on and on about 'professionals making such a mess' and 'the language'. 'Who pays for it all?' 'Why was Sugar allowed on site? He was a danger!' and then Danny started complained about me giving Dirty Gertie to Sugar. He went on and on until I agreed that next time I was in the pound shop I would replace her. Pretty Penny went on and on: 'Who is footing the bill for that? We are, that's who, and it's going to cost a pretty penny', which is how she got her name. I was glad to see them make their way back to their plots.

As Pretty Penny was leaving she couldn't help herself. 'Haven't seen your friend lately?', nodding in the direction of Kitty's plot. There was that smirk again. Mick started off down the path whilst Penny continued, 'Have we, Mick? Not seen

Kitty?' Mick ignored her and carried on walking. Smiling to herself, she got up and started to follow him. She wasn't the kind of person I would readily sit in company with, but on the allotments you take what you have around you and make the best of it. Danny commented on the two of them walking away. 'Man, I would na 'a that from any woman.'

Danny was English with a Jamaican father and a Yorkshire mother. He had a strong Yorkshire accent but with a stronger Jamaican lilt. It was the strangest of sounds: the Jamaican sang words and sentences at you, going up and down the scales, but the words were all heavy, flat Yorkshire words.

Danny went to inspect the damage caused by Sugar and his rescuers. I started to tidy the cups away whilst studying my list of jobs written on the chalkboard on the back of my shed door (I used to call it a blackboard but when Danny moved next to me he decided that it was politically incorrect to say "blackboard" so now I refer to it as a "chalkboard") and was trying to decide which of the jobs to do next.

Danny, at the best of times, was not a pretty sight: he was early sixties, stood at about six foot, was extremely thin with very few teeth in situ, and dark sunken eyes, his hair a mixture of grey and white pulled up in wool strands of many colours. The arrogant, cock sure, laughing Danny had been replaced by a nervous, twitching, dreadlock-wearing skull. He waved a piece of paper and some red and white tape in the air, shouting, using similar language to that he had been complaining about earlier. 'They are telling me to demolish my shed, bastards, and they're coming back, they're coming back to check.' The ranting and raving continued until Danny left to go home to phone a list of people he was going to complain to, from the local MP to the papers, the council—the list went on.

I worked until lunchtime feeling so sorry about Sugar, then giggling to myself about Danny's shed, I wondered if Kitty would come today, not only to tell her the early morning activities, but also that I was looking forward to our trip. We were planning to get some chickens as soon as spring arrived, but first we needed to buy a coop.

I went home to write to my daughter and tell her about the tales from the plot. She and her husband are convinced that our allotments are just a cover for growing marijuana, illicitly distilling booze, sex and debauchery. It is true, we have had instances, and more, but not on a daily basis—and not in my shed.

Me and My Allotment

I took over the allotment when Harry passed away six years ago. Initially I did it because he loved it and I wanted to try and keep something of him alive. Now I enjoy it and it gives me a reason to get up each day and there is a level of responsibility. I *have* to water or I *have* to weed, and it has the added benefit of being seen. Before I took the allotment, I didn't really take much notice of the changing seasons, they just came and went. Now I find great pleasure in looking forward to the beginning of a season, each one bringing changes, new challenges and jobs to do around the plot, plus the company of likeminded people. Here we are, thrown together with a common goal: to grow crops. Some, like me, take up an allotment because they need to do something constructive with their time. Others do it because of the fresh, healthy vegetables it gives, some for the exercise and fresh air, some to escape the other half. Either way, it makes for a varied and diverse community that for few hours each day comes together, separately but with a common goal, and like all communities you can't pick and choose the people included.

I didn't bargain for old age. I don't feel old. And what's more, I refuse to be old. When people refer to me as "old" I am shocked; I may be a bit wrinkly but I am not old-old. It didn't even occur to me until I heard those famous words that were used when Harry died: 'well, he was an age'. Yes, we are one age or another. And 'well, he had a good innings'. What is a good innings? 100 not out, I'd say.

Very few people can see old people, and if they can it is because their own old age is rapidly approaching and an element of panic is setting it, they can see their future. The major part of society looks on you as though you have been old all your life: that you were born old, have no life experiences, no notion of youth, careers, love, family, and treat you at best as an inconvenience—and the saddest of all, that you have nothing to contribute to today's young, modern society.

I often wonder where they think we came from. Maybe made in a strange human development factory that is supposed to be turning out young people with smooth skin, sparkling teeth and eyes, with flawless complexions and brains that know *absolutely everything*, when one day the machine malfunctioned, turning out rejects with skin too big for the bodies, making it fall in folds and wrinkles, with limbs that don't work, toothless, with white hair and obviously knowing *nothing*. Before they knew it, they were churning out thousands of rejects, calling them "the old". And when they got tired of throwing all "the old" into skips at the back of the factory, they decided to open the factory doors and let them wander off with the warnings "keep out of sight", "try not to get in the way or want too much". We are the rejects, "the old", and allotments are where we hang out.

On the allotment there is an assumption that we single old ladies have automatic knowledge of pruning roses and growing flowers and food for the table, therefore we know all about gardens and growing vegetables. Who am I with newly found status to upset them and tell them that I haven't got a clue? I am not invisible on the allotments; in fact, I am positively welcomed and can be seen! I hang my cloak of invisibility on the allotment gate and enter the land of the old.

It was Kitty that cajoled me into joining the committee as she was the only female member. Before I knew it, I was nominated, seconded, and became part of the much hated and much maligned committee. It's better than being invisible. Kitty isn't "the old" but is rapidly approaching "the old" and is trying to prepare herself.

I live in a small bungalow within walking distance of the allotment. I still have Harry's car but only use it once or twice a week for shopping or going to visit friends. Soon after Harry died, my son-in-law, Alan, was made redundant. Fortunately, he was offered a job in Australia and within weeks my daughter, Emma, along with Alan and my lovely granddaughter, Megan, were gone. Initially the contract was for two years, which seemed a long time, but it went quite quickly. After a further two years, I didn't think they would be coming back. I couldn't blame them; it looks a beautiful country and they have a good life, a lovely home and Megan, aged twelve, had settled in school and was doing very well. I longed to visit them and was trying to save the fare. I say 'trying' as each time I amassed a few hundred something happened and I had to use it to buy a new washing machine or pay the heating bill after a very cold winter. Now my daughter wanted me to buy a computer so we could *Skype*! I had priced computers and a laptop thing was suggested, but they are very expensive, and I didn't know what Skype was except that we would be able to see each other and talk, which would be lovely just to see them and my lovely Megan.

If I sold the bungalow I could go to visit them, but Harry and I worked to save up for the deposit, then worked so hard to pay off the mortgage, doing without holidays and luxuries for years; it seemed selfish now to sell it and use the money for a holiday without him. And where would I live when I got back? No, I would continue to save and hope that no major bills or repairs came in until I had the money for my holiday. I worked out that with the fare plus a one-night stopover to get a night's sleep there and back (so I wouldn't be too tired when I arrived), staying for a month with Emma and Alan, and taking into consideration spends—I so wanted to spoil my Megan too—I would need about £3,000 to £3,500. It had taken me two years to save £500, so at a rate of £500 in two years, it would take me another ten to twelve years and then I would be 78!!

There's always the lottery, of course. And as an allotment committee member, I was asked to join the committee syndicate and had been donating £8 each month by direct debit for the past couple of years to the site secretary, John Farthing, who did it magically through the internet. As of yet, it's just the odd lucky dip. I wouldn't be holding my breath.

I have been watching one of those antiques shows about raising money from forgotten items in the attic or cellar and putting them up for sale in an auction house. It gave me the idea to raise money in the same way, so I started checking out the attic and looking about the house for items I hadn't used and had forgotten about. I felt quite excited.

I came up with two boxes, including old trains, a dinner service, some Toby jugs of an ugly pirate, and two old paintings. I rang the local auctioneer. He explained in his strong Scottish accent that they had a minimum fee of £10 and then 20% commission on the hammer price. He didn't seem impressed and in a very dour Scottish accent told me 'you'll be lucky to get £20' but to bring them in on a Wednesday for the following Monday auction and he would split them into lots. I lost my enthusiasm. Twenty pounds! I left the "lots" in the dining room, closed the door and went to the land of "the old".

Corner George was the only one there, working away in his greenhouse. George was in his eighties, a war veteran. I often stop to speak to George; he is quiet, interesting and good humoured. He was sent to Italy, landing in Sicily with the invasion force to take Italy, who by then had signed up with Germany. He rarely spoke about the war but on the rare occasions he did, he said 'God forgive me for the things I had to do'. His sorrow was palpable, even now, nearly sixty years on. Another was 'When we arrived in Italy, the locals spat at us in the street. When the war had finished and we were leaving, they offered us their women, we spat at them'.

He hated three things: Italians, war and German Shepherd dogs.

I stopped to talk to Corner George to see how his carrots were coming along. Carrots are difficult to grow: I have tried them in containers, boxes, baths, straight in the ground, in the greenhouse, under cloches with little success. Some grow to a couple of inches and then the carrot fly gets them. The common misnomer is that planting them in containers or raised beds about 18 inches off the ground means the carrot fly can't fly that high to get them. Someone should have told the carrot fly of its limitations. It's utter tosh—they can and do. Corner George has the touch and his carrots never fail, which is very irritating. George has been growing and showing his carrots for years. He and John Farthing win all the prizes for onions and carrots at the site vegetable show every year. They are in competition with each other more than anyone in the show and no one else comes near their success. This year, Kitty and I have decided we are going to enter and have been planning what to grow and when to plant so they will be at their best by the time of the show. I relayed this to George, telling him we were going to knock him and John off the winners' list this year. George took it in good heart, saying he loves a challenge. He told me how he mixes the soil he grows his carrots in. If you are going to grow show carrots and parsnips, use pipes, three feet deep, and place one or two seeds in each. He showed me his rows of pipes all ready for sowing. I hoped Kitty was on the plot so I could pass on all this information before I forgot it. I had lots of news to tell.

I finally moved on down the lane, putting my head down as I passed John Farthing OBE who was working on his plot. Sadly he saw me, and he never misses an opportunity to have a go. 'Wait there, I want a word with you,' he muttered.

According to John Farthing, his history includes being a qualified chartered accountant and getting his OBE by doing years as a missionary in Africa.

When I asked Harry about the people on the plots, he found good in them all except for John Farthing. He said he was a devious shit-stirrer of a man who should not be trusted and never should have been appointed as site secretary or treasurer. He only got on because of the casting vote from the vicar. Evidently, John attends his church and does odd jobs, gardening

31

and tidying, helps with the "bring and buy" sales, does the evening service collections and is so helpful at the funerals, etc. He also casts doubt on his OBE.

As I stood by his gate, his old Labrador started to waddle up the path towards me, wagging his tail. I could see the back of John bending over a large metal drum full of water. I leaned over to pat the dog as he appeared. 'Get in that shed!' he shouted. I wasn't sure if he meant me but the dog shot into the shed. He grunted and walked in my direction, dangling something between his finger and thumb. As he got closer, I could see it: he was holding a rat by its tail, water was dripping off its long nose, it was struggling, trying to escape. 'Yesterday, I should have been called. I *am* the site secretary, you know,' he snarled. I couldn't stop looking at the rat—it was mortified with fear, as was I. I could feel my mouth starting to get dry. 'I am going to have him thrown off my site, he is a bloody nuisance and it's him that's starting the fires and all the vandalism, that's him, you know?'

I tried to speak, but he interrupted. As he spoke, the soaking wet rat bobbed up and down, waving from side to side, his massive terrified eyes staring at me. I started to feel faint. 'If anything else happens, you call me first. As site secretary I should be the first to know and I can deal with it *properly*!'

Inferring that I hadn't dealt with it *properly*, I was regretting having spoken to him as he continued his rant. He leaned on his fence with both hands. I could hear the rat scratching the fence, trying to get a foothold on the wood. 'Keep still, you dirty little bastard!' he shouted at the rat. 'He should have been drowned at birth too, would have saved a few sheds.' He used the hand holding the rat to point at me to ram home his point. I felt sick, I must have lost colour. 'Don't like rats, ay?' he said, lifting it up higher for me to see. 'Caught her and her brood in me trap this morning, six of the little buggers, there swimming with the fishes now,' he sniggered, 'and you're going for a swim too, aren't you?' he said, looking the rat in the eye. 'The little ones are still weak and just wriggle a bit, but mummy here, well, she puts up a fight. I have to hold her down or she'll be off. Don't know where the old fella is, but I'll find him. Don't you worry, dear, he will be joining you soon.' I felt nauseous. 'How is your mate? Haven't seen her for a while. I hear she is having man trouble too. He got away?' He was giving me one of his lecherous smiles, displaying his few brown tombstone teeth, allowing me privy to his cigarette breath. I stammered that I thought she was spring cleaning. 'That's what they call it now?' He laughed heartily at the joke that only he understood; he rocked back and forth with laughter, the poor rat's eyes bulging in terror, swinging and bobbing up and

down as John enjoyed his hilarious joke. I was glad to get
away.

I made a noise that sounded like 'must go' and turned, taking
two steps, when I heard a loud noise and his scream. He was
lying face down on his path; mummy rat moved like lightening
across the lane to safety, the dog whimpered with fright. John
hadn't noticed that the dog had snuck out of the shed and was
lying behind him on the path. He was then on his knees, going
red-faced, trying to pull his great bulk up with the aid of his
gate, shouting, 'She bit me, the bloody thing bit me!' I looked
at his cheek and there, quite clearly, were two holes where
mummy rat had sunk her very sharp front teeth and the blood
was dripping down his face. 'You should get to the hospital
with that,' I suggested, but he insisted he was okay. Good
mummy rat, I thought—then the devil got me. I regaled him of
a tale I'd made up in an instant.
'You should go to hospital, John, or you could get Lemon's
Disease!'
'Lemon's Disease? Never heard of it!'
I proceeded, 'My friend, Mavis, well her husband was very ill
and taken into the hospital. He was in for weeks and they
didn't know what was up with him, but he couldn't walk,
could hardly breathe, and couldn't even go the loo without

34

help. He was delirious, kept trying to get into bed with some of the old ladies. He had to be restrained. They tested him for everything and couldn't find out what it was. Anyway, they brought in the tropical diseases people and they tested him for malaria, spider bites and every infection under the sun. They narrowed it down to his prostate, so they shoved a camera right up his . . .', pointing to my backside, '. . . then they thought it was internal bleeding from the bowels so they shoved the camera right up his . . .'

John was on his feet, wiping his face and glaring at the dog who now decided the shed was the best place to be. 'And . . .?' he said, getting annoyed.

'Well, they asked if he had been in contact with vermin and he said no. Oh, he was in a bad way, couldn't eat, sweating, coughing, wetting himself, ooh the smell . . . it was bad. In the end, they called his wife to come in so they could tell her the bad news that they didn't know what it was, that they were at a loss. They suggested that they get the priest he was that bad. They didn't know what was causing it, you see, if they know what causes it, they can deal with it but they didn't so . . .'

He was getting redder and redder and the blood kept flowing down his cheek and onto the fence that was supporting him. 'For God's sake woman, get to the point!'

'When they spoke to Mavis, that's his wife, they asked her about being in contact with vermin and she said 'like mice?' and they said 'yes' so she said 'yes, look at his right calf' and there it was!'

'What was?'

'The bite mark.'

'A mouse had bitten him?'

'No.'

'What then?'

'A rat.'

'And s . . .?'

'You get Lemon's Disease from rats. I knew that—Harry told me they lived in fear of it in the army. She'd saved his life, made him realise how precious life is, he said. He would be forever grateful to her, he said, then took off with his fancy piece. Ooh, Mavis was cross. If she hadn't told them about the bite, she would be on a world cruise now with the insurance money . . . I'd go the hospital and tell them you need a tetanus injection cos you have Lemon's Disease.'

Delighted to get away, I looked to see if I could see mummy rat. I had a mental picture of her sitting somewhere saying 'lovely to see Karma in action'.

I walked slowly to my plot, sat in my shed for a few minutes to control my nerves. I absolutely hate rats, but what a dreadful way to die, and her babies. I was horrified and confused. I went over what he said about Kitty. John Farthing is known for his idle gossip and when he has none, he creates a story to suit his mood. He has been known to deliberately cause "situations" just to watch the players react. Fingers crossed for Lyme's Disease.

Kitty and I were supposed to be meeting to discuss this coming Sunday's monthly committee meeting agenda which was always the same: site security, site secretary's update, vandalism, state of the paths, especially after a wet winter, and ideas for raising money. Today was a bit different though, and we were supposed to be meeting up to discuss the agenda. But I needed to go home; I hoped that today would be a quiet day after the stress of Sugar yesterday but no, I felt dirty and stressed and I needed to have another shower and to lie down . . . and it was only 8.30 am!

The Crims

As I arrived at my shed a week later on a lovely spring morning, I noticed the bolt was different, not quite closed properly.
This usually meant one of two things: One, I had visitors in the
night, or two, lovely fresh honey. I stopped locking my shed
after the fifth break-in. They rarely take anything but break the
door or window in an effort to get in to discover you have
nothing of value. Bobby Bee (real name Robert Johnson)
keeps beehives behind John Farthing's plot. He keeps them
close to the wall at the furthest end of the site in an effort to
give his bees as much flying space between the hive and John.
The council allows the keeping of bees, rabbits and chickens
which means John just has to simmer with rage and can't do
anything about them, although any sign of someone being
stung by *any* insect results in Bobby getting an earful from
John. Needless to say, John doesn't get any honey. The honey
is lovely so I swap my strawberry jam for Bobby's honey.
Bobby is also a fellow member of the allotment committee.
Fortunately, on this occasion, it was the honey.

I suppose the keeping of rabbits stems back to the war when
meat was hard to come by, and rabbits are good meat. Now if

any one sees a rabbit on site, it's a major alert as they can devastate a garden in a few hours.

Chickens are kept for eggs; no cockerels are to be kept at all under any circumstances—as Jock and Pat did (now known as "The Crims"). Let's say you go to a farm and buy six chicks, all lovely and fluffy, looking sweet, keeping them indoors for a while, handfeeding them, watching them grow, having little play fights to establish the pecking order. Then one morning, a letter from the council arrives, informing you that you cannot keep cockerels: quite a shock when you thought they were hens. Evidently, they have to grow for a few months before they can determine their sex. These were definitely cockerels from the noise they have been making in the very early morning—waking and annoying the neighbours confirmed that—and they must be disposed of with immediate effect.

One morning, not long after that, the chickens were gone. I was told that they had been taken back to the farmer and that The Crims were devastated and never wanted any more chickens and would like to sell his chicken paraphernalia at a knockdown price. I was delighted to help and couldn't wait to tell Kitty. This meant we could get the chicks sooner than expected and we wouldn't make any mistakes—well, not that one anyway. With the help of his fellow Crim, they moved it all onto my plot that day and we helped them build the necessary fox-proof fence. They even gave us the boxes they were transported in. We were delighted. I couldn't believe our good fortune and was looking forward to getting the "girls". There was no mention at this stage of the antics that had gone on the night before.

When the policemen arrived the following day, they walked round the site looking for people who kept chickens or had a coop. I was one of the first people they came to, enquiring where our chickens were. The younger of the two was about five foot four, thin, looked like his mum had given him a good scrub not a minute before, he had pale skin with freckles mixed with spots, and definitely had never needed a razor blade. I decided I needed to keep quiet about where we got the coop, from explaining that we hadn't got our girls yet but would be getting rescue hens as soon as they were available. I did play the little old lady card as best I could: asking him to have a cup of tea; when they asked did I have a ladder, 'why do you want a ladder, are you going scrumping?'; when they enquired about an empty coop, I pushed some rhubarb on them both; 'No girls yet, we are going to rescue some . . .'; a lettuce from the greenhouse as they continued to protest that they

40

couldn't take them; '. . . going to rescue some from a farm with batteries.' He also asked about the "Keep Out Dangerous" sign and tape around Danny's plot. I explained as best as a little old lady can, telling him about Sugar, Dirty Gertie and the fire brigade. They were glad to get away, talking quietly as they walked down the path with rhubarb and lettuce. I heard Freckles say, 'Poor old bugger . . . can't see her trying to lob chickens over a fence, can you?'

The tale of the master Criminals gets embroidered with each airing, but it is true that the sanctuary alarms went off and the police arrived. And they did have chickens that turned out to be cockerels and they did disappear overnight . . . and he does make the most excellent loopy juice! The tale goes like this:

One lazy spring evening, sitting in his shed, bemoaning his misfortune to his fellow allotmenteer and sampling last year's homebrewed rhubarb wine (AKA loopy juice), the cockerel owner was naturally very upset. He thought he had hens and was so looking forward to fresh eggs, he had spent a fortune on the coop, food, and bedding, not to mention the cost of the chickens. The "play fights" he put down to high jinks, not six very territorial cockerels locked together in mortal combat—a few more weeks and it would have been like a war zone. He

41

was going to have a word with the farmer who sold them. But he knew that if he took them back, it would be into a pot for his chickens, and he couldn't do that, nor could he do the dastardly deed of wringing their necks. He then decided upon a plan and co-opted his fellow drinker to assist.

After a walk to the Castel Road Animal and Pet Sanctuary (nicknamed CRAPs), the two agreed that the cockerels would probably fit through the bars of the wrought iron gate, and if not could be thrown over the top. They returned to the plot, boxed all the cockerels up in two cardboard boxes, refreshed their thirst with another glass of homebrew, placed the boxes in the wheelbarrow and set off again for the gate. After several attempts at shoving the birds through the bars of the gate, the cockerels refusing to cooperate and breathe in so they could be squeezed through, they tried the second plan. After several attempts of throwing the birds *over* the gate, they realised they couldn't throw high enough—they had underestimated the height of the gates and the birds just kept hitting the gate two thirds of the way up and sliding down in stunned silence. An effort was made to catch them as they slid down the gate, resulting in further scaring the living daylights out of the birds, then on hitting the ground, the cockerels gathered their screeching vocals, let rip and bolted for it. The master Criminals managed to stumble on them and wrestle them back into the boxes before piling them into the wheelbarrow. Abandoning this idea, they went back to the shed to rethink their plan.

Refreshed with yet more loopy juice to fortify them, the third idea was formed: a more realistic plan requiring the use of a ladder! The birds had been put back in their coop and, having had a harrowing day, had already gone into roost, making them very easy to deal with. After further fortification, which by now was being hailed as his best vintage, they pushed the cockerels back into each box again. They pinched a twelve-foot ladder from a neighbouring plot and, with the ladder and two boxes of cockerels perched in a wheelbarrow, set off down the six-foot-wide lane with its hawthorn hedges either side to CRAPS once again. The evening was drawing in now, getting colder and darker, which made walking down the lane more difficult. After several attempts of trying to wobble down the six-foot-wide lane, with the twelve-foot-wide ladder perched across the wheelbarrow getting entangled with the prickly hawthorn hedge, both Crims were being ripped to shreds whilst trying to remove it. Eventually, Crim 1 suggested that Crim 2 should carry the ladder to prevent this happening and again they set off down the lane to CRAPS, with Crim 1 pushing the wheelbarrow in which sat the boxes of now noisy, un-happy birds.

On reaching the gate of the sanctuary, the befuddled half-cut Crims managed to erect the ladder without beheading each other. They placed the ladder on one side of the big double iron gates. Crim 1 was to climb the ladder and, keeping to health and safety guidelines directed by Crim 1, Crim 2 was to foot the ladder, handing up the first box at the appropriate moment. Crim 1 got two thirds of the way up and Crim 2 handed him one box of cockerels, the idea being to empty the contents over the other side so the birds would just float into the sanctuary.

The sanctuary gates were very old and needed oiling; they moved under the weight of the ladder, Crim 1 and a box of noisy cockerels. The gate made the kind of creaking noise that came straight out of the *Hammer House of Horror*. Fortunate-ly, it stopped, and checking no one had heard the noise, they tittered and continued to the top of the ladder. Crim 1 began to open the box to drop the cockerels over the other side.

It was a good old-fashioned bell that started to ring out first, then floodlights came on, lighting up the gate, the whole yard and Crim 1 up the ladder. They do say that once chickens go to roost, you can move them without them making a noise, but not these cockerels—these were screaming at full pelt. The motion of the panicking hens in the box made them shake and vibrate in Crim 1's arms, at which point they started to escape, continuing with the unholy din. As he shook with fear, Crim 1 began to lose his grip on the box. They were trying to escape. He grabbed the first escapee and quickly threw it over the gate, but in the effort to do so, he had to let go of the box which fell back into the wheelbarrow, upsetting the other box. The bell was blasting out and the lights could be seen from Mars. All five cockerels escaped, running in panic in different directions.

Instinctively, one of the half-cut pensioners set off in pursuit. The second tried to dismount the ladder at speed, causing him to stumble off the last few rungs. He followed his follow Criminal accomplice, first chasing one cockerel, then another, then another, until five minutes later they gave up, exhausted, and walked back for the ladder and wheelbarrow. The bells were still blaring out but not enough to hide the police sirens. With a quick look at each other, they speedily grabbed their equipment and ran into the lane. They stood and watched from the darkness of the lane: they could see the gate and the Panda cars come to a screaming halt, officers on radios asking for permission to enter the premises to turn the alarms off.

Police dogs jumped out of the back of a van, growling and barking. The dog handlers couldn't hold the dogs back; they ran at the gates, throwing themselves against them, trying to get in. The police dogs were desperate to get in; they were barking, leaping up, frothing at the mouth, bearing their teeth and growling at the enemy.

The cockerel, standing fearless and proud, strutted from one side of the gate to the other, wings flapping, comb up, neck high, head bobbing, squawking at the top of his voice, threatening the dogs. The dogs were beyond rage, trying to dig their way in, then racing from side to side to try and find a way in. The police handlers were hanging on the back of the leads, trying to control them. The loopy juice drinkers backed away quietly, leaving the pandemonium they had created.

Bees, on the other hand, are far less bother; they make honey and behave well—until they swarm and we all have to run to our greenhouses and lock ourselves in until they have settled. 'Bad beekeeping,' Bobby had said, until one day *his* bees swarmed all over John Farthing's plot . . . dear me, John wasn't happy, nor was Bobby—he said a swarm he had collected the previous month must have had some rogue bees from a bad part of town in them and taught all the nice bees to be naughty. We laughed at this until we heard that rogue bees can create a nasty hive which can chase people and sting them. The previous summer, on a very hot day, one lady plot holder who had been chased by naughty bees ended up locked in her greenhouse. She had left her phone in the shed and was too scared to come out—sat there until someone came to look for her, by which time she was virtually stripped naked and dehydrated. The hive was destroyed and replaced with a new, well-behaved colony that makes the very best honey.

Kitty

Allotments are microcosms of society and, as such, have people that gossip about anything and everything; some of it has foundations and some not. When gossip started about Kitty, I decided to find out one way or another.

I rang Kitty a good few times and was about to give up, but the comments that had been made lately made me wonder if she was worried about coming up. Did she think people were talking about her? What if she *did* have a man friend? Nothing wrong with that. And if her friends give up that easily, are they really friends? It was only about two miles away, so I walked to her house. Kit is a redhead, with long strands of red hair tied up in various scarves. In her youth, she would have been quite striking; now in her fifties, still attractive. I think the hair has helped to maintain the colour. She is a funny, confident, individual woman, she always wears red lipstick and long, flowing type skirts, could hold her own at the society meetings and would correct all those around her if she thought they were wrong. The thought of her being upset by gossip didn't fit somehow. She appeared to be pretty thick-skinned and would probably be happy to give them all a mouthful, but then, do you ever really know people?

At first, I didn't think she was going to answer the door. I knew she was in, or at least her car was in the drive and I could see her "summer transport", her bike, in the hall. I was just about to leave when she opened the door and asked me in. When we got in, she made a cup of tea and we sat in the lounge talking. I told her all about Sugar and we both felt awful about taking the mickey out of him and decided that we would go and see him in hospital.

Kitty was more IT savvy than me, not a high bar, I know. She had a printout of the society agenda which was organised for the coming Sunday. We discussed some of the issues we knew would come up. Kitty's phone buzzed twice whilst I was there. She just said, 'PPI again.'

Kitty also showed me how computers work and suggested I would benefit from Skype and showed me how it worked. To do this she visited YouTube. I had never seen any of these things before and, although Kitty kept saying she didn't have much of a clue what she was doing, I was fascinated. It was all too quick—I wanted her to slow down. However, she managed to convince me that I should have a computer and go to lessons to learn how to use one properly. I was in awe of this machine that could do anything and knew everything. I decided it would be wiser to spend my £500 on a computer so I could see and talk to my daughter and granddaughter in Queensland, as I felt sure I would never be able to raise enough money to visit them. I shared this with Kitty and she agreed and suggested that I needed help, and although Kitty was more IT savvy than me, she wasn't the one to advise me and suggested I spoke to one of "The Cowboys". The mobile buzzed again. I suggested she answered it but she just said, 'It'll just be PPI.'

After showing me how Skype worked, we looked at another amazing part of the computer: the allotment Facebook page, seeing all the comments and pictures and jokes. I realised it was like a layer of communication that carried on in a mystical world without me. If I needed convincing any further, that was it. There were comments from Danny about Sugar with some embellishments of his own. John Farthing couldn't resist snide comments about Kitty's absence from the allotment. There was a little box that popped up in the corner, and as I started to read it, Kitty pressed something and it disappeared. I didn't get all the sentence but it started with 'I am looking forward' and that was all I got. Kitty looked upset and said, 'You might as well

know, everyone else seems to know. I have been seeing Mike.'
I sat blankly in silence while I tried to work out who Mike
was. Fat Mick.

When I left her house, I was glad I had walked there; I needed
the exercise home to get my head around what she had said.
Kitty and Mick—Fat Mick.

The tale went that Mick, Penny and Kitty had gone to the same
school and for a while Mick and Kitty went out together until
they parted, going their separate ways: Mick to an apprentice-
ship and Kitty to university to study art in Leeds. Mick went
into the local ship yard until it was closed five years ago. Both
married, Kitty quickly divorced her husband and never ventured again, Mick married and settled down with Pretty Penny.

Mick and Kitty met for the first time since school on the allotment and became good friends, just having cups of tea and
talking about the past and people they went to school with.
They talked about planting and growing and the normal lotty
chatter. At that stage, Pretty Penny didn't come down to the
plot, wasn't interested, didn't want to be out all day in the dirt.
But something must have caught her attention, maybe it was
Mick spending more time there, or maybe he just looked too

51

happy. A few weeks later, Pretty Penny turned up at the allotment open day and saw Mick and Kitty working together on the tombola stall, laughing. We didn't see Mick or Penny for about a month after that. Then Penny started coming down on her own, saying how much she loved her plot and how she can't get Mick to come down any more. Then, whispering as if it was a big secret she was sharing, she said things like 'I think someone has upset him!' 'He doesn't like coming down anymore.' 'It's not right they should be thrown off for bullying!

Then, as suddenly as it had stopped, they both started to come down together and that is how it has been—Fat Mick and Pretty Penny always together, sometimes just Penny but never just Mick.

Sometimes, Penny would insist that she and Mick went over to see Kitty and would tell Mick to help with jobs on her plot whilst she just stood and watched, at times shouting at Mick and telling him he was so stupid for doing something wrong or just staring at them both, watching.

Kitty clicked back on the box in the corner—it was from Pretty Penny. As Kitty clicked on it, it revealed lots of messages from Penny, swinging from how happy she and Mick were to Mick being a terrible husband and that she didn't blame Kitty, it was all him . . . how she wanted the three of them to be friends and that's why she made Mick help her. Then to say how lovely Kitty looked on this particular day, then to how lucky she was and then straight to what a happy marriage she had. What an odd bod! There was certainly an element of instability there.

A while later, one morning, Mick and Kitty bumped into each other coming out of the doctors'. At first it was very awkward, neither knowing what to say. They went for a coffee and Kitty apologised for creating problems for him—she thought that he was keeping away because she had upset him. Mick was very embarrassed about the way Penny was behaving and decided keeping away would give her time to settle. From then on, they met quite regularly. They both felt a bit mischievous doing this but kept it up, nonetheless, until it changed to a drink once in a while, when he could make a reasonable excuse. Then he went to a golf weekend. Mick didn't spend all the time on the green. A year ago, they had decided to stop as they both felt it was just finishing off their school relationship, so decided to leave it at that.

They had seen each other on the allotment but just kept to nodding and smiling at each other. Nothing else happened until a few months after when they accidently met again at the supermarket and decided to have a catch-up cup of coffee in full view of the public in the supermarket café. They were seen together by Pretty Penny's sister, who duly reported the incident to Penny. Since then, Pretty Penny has pestered Kitty, sending texts, sending messages on Facebook, following her in the street, sitting, just spending hours at the allotment watching her. One minute Penny would come over to speak to her, as nice as pie, the next she would walk away and come back spitting quiet but vicious abuse. So Kitty became worn out by it all and didn't know what to do, even considered giving up her allotment. She hasn't seen Mick since or spoken to him, but wondering how he was faring. The only thing I could say was 'hen pecked'!

My only lame suggestion was that Kitty should come back, and whenever she is there we would be together. If Pretty Penny continued we would call the police and from now on Kitty should keep a diary of these events.

When I got home, I tried to remember the things Kitty had done on the computer and made notes of the things I wanted to ask "The Cowboys" about. I was totally unfamiliar with the terminology: new words that I had never heard of, no idea of how it worked, but I was going to find out if it meant that I could see and talk to my granddaughter. But first I had to learn all about the internet, skypes and facetubes. I was waiting for "The Cowboys".

The Meeting

The society meeting was on a Saturday morning and was to last about an hour, 10 am until 11 am. There were eight committee members including myself, Kitty, the vicar and John Farthing plus the other four easy-going men trying to help plot holders. Tea and coffee are always the first thing to delay the start of the meeting, then general chit chat. After about half an hour of wasted time, someone would insist we get on with the agenda. This day the meeting started at 10.35 am.

It was a lovely morning and I resented attending a meeting, knowing that we cover the same ground each time, making little or no progress and usually end up in disagreement. It takes so long to make a decision, it's a wonder anything ever gets done.

We usually went through the long list of complaints, ending up with John losing his temper, blaming everyone but himself, and if someone actually stood up to him he would divert the aggressor by suggesting they themselves did the dastardly deed. As was the case at this meeting.

Prior to most meetings, Kitty and I met and had a wander around the site just to talk to other plot holders in an effort to see if they wanted to make constructive comments or contribute any ideas to the site so we could include them in the meeting. This didn't always go to plan. Quite often, after asking a plot holder for their contribution, we are met with a high level of abuse. Today was one of those days: 'The society couldn't run around in a circle successfully.' 'You're just glorified, jumped-up Hitlers.' 'A load of tossers.' 'Useless! Couldn't stop a pig in a jigger, any of you.' We became hardened to most of those negative types of comments but today we heard a new one, and we didn't much like it.

Today we thought we would pick Corner George's brain on carrot growing and as we did, we asked for his contribution to the running of the site.

After some discussion about carrot growing, types of carrots, how they are measured in competition—not as straight forward as one would think!—George, being the very pleasant man that he is, gave us all kinds of insights into growing carrots. But when asked about contributing to the meeting, he declined to answer. However, after some of Kitty's feline persuasion, he said it was just that rumours had been circulating around the site for some time and we must know about it: That we were 'all on the fiddle' and that we just raised money and kept it for ourselves. We were stunned, as every penny was accounted for, we all checked the books, had receipts for everything—it was as clean as a whistle. No one could *fiddle*—it was all done by the book. We explained to George that the accounts were open for all plot holders to view at any time. He was clearly uneasy and felt he shouldn't have said anything, said that he would not be drawn any further into it. We were at a loss to understand what this referred too.

Like two schoolgirls with exciting news, we hotfooted it to the meeting, talking as we went: had either of us heard this before? No. Had any of the committee? It certainly hadn't come up as far as we knew. We felt that this should be item number one on the agenda today.

As no one wanted to pick up the "chair mantel"—we have a rolling chair, that is, each meeting has a different committee member as chair—as unluck would have it, today was John's turn. Never a nice meeting when he chairs. And when we actually got down to the agenda at 10.35 am, time and time again we tried to raise the issue that rumour had it we, the committee, were on the fiddle, but time and time again the chair told us to bring it up under AOB (any other business).

It was 11.30 am before AOB came up and then he closed the meeting, asking us to have the matter included on the agenda for next month. As usual, committee members took off to their homes or plots, leaving John Farthing, Kitty and myself. We explained to John what had been said and that we should give every plot holder a copy of the accounts to ensure they under-stood there was nothing underhanded going on.

In hindsight, which is always very knowledgeable, we were very stupid and shouldn't have mentioned it then—as attack is the best form of defence and he took it. He became aggressive, stomping up and down, shouting about everything in his wake, saying we should spend more time concerning ourselves with our plot and our personal behaviour before questioning anyone else's. He stomped away, shouting abuse back at us, saying that we never contributed to the committee and if we wanted to do the accounts we could, he was sick of us all, all he wanted to do was help the plot holders and we always stood in his way. We were glad he was gone.

Kitty and I were left bewildered. Plot holders thought we were on the fiddle. Why did John carry on like a madman if plot holders were saying we were dishonest? It must have come up before—had we missed something at a meeting? We had seen the accounts and they were fine, so why did he get so upset? It was obviously just a nasty rumour that needed to be dealt with by the committee; if we could ever get a word in edgeways at the meetings we could help sort it out. John's behaviour was a mystery, horrid man, but this time he had nothing to worry about.

The weather was overcast now and threatening rain. Kitty and I made a cup of tea in my shed and discussed getting our hens. We had found a farmer who was about to slaughter his hens and was happy to sell them off cheap. They had reached the end of their useful life, their egg production was slowing down, therefore they would be slaughtered if he couldn't find a home for them. We had enough room for about ten but agreed six would be a better number and give them more room to play. Just then, I thought I heard my gate creak and waited for a face to appear at the door. Nothing.

We both worked on our plots for a couple of hours. It was still too early to plant most things so I spent my time cleaning the greenhouses and lighting the sulphur candles to kill off any insects or pests from last year. The smell from cleaning the glass with Jeyes Fluid takes me back to when I was a girl and my mum used it to clean the kitchen floor, mixed with the smell of the washing bubbling away in the boiler. After a few days have passed and the smell of the candle has done its job I can start the very exciting job of sowing some early lettuce and cabbage.

Each year as the growing season comes to an end, the next couple of months are about tidying, repairing and preparing for the next spring. There is so much to do in these winter months, including planting out onions and garlic. And if, like me, you like your greens throughout the winter, planting kale, spinach and purple sprouting broccoli. But most of it is about preparing for the next growing season. What will you grow? Where will you plant it? What was grown in that bed this year and what can follow it? I'll make a plan!

In January, seed potatoes are in the shops. This is such an exciting time; it marks the start of the season and spring is so close. You start to see fellow allotmenteers again. They have spent winter rugged up against the cold, showing just a pair of eyes and a red, dripping nose, working in sheds or greenhouses. But as the days draw out, they come earlier, go later, work outside, showing hair and hands that have been covered all winter. Spring comes with the same inevitable chatter that is repeated several times a day with whoever you talk to but you never get tired of: 'What have you put in?' 'Isn't that a bit early/late?' 'I am not doing that this year' or 'I am going to try that this year' or 'Oh, my potatoes were awful last year, full of eelworm'. To which the lotty elders (those who have been there for years and years and have tried everything) reply: 'You need to cover the bed with lime before winter and then a month before you rake plenty of potash in'.

The amount of differing opinions is vast. There are two schools of thought on covering beds to help stop weeds growing in early spring: 'The slugs and weeds are delighted with black weed fabric cover as you are keeping them warm for the winter and they are stronger in spring' versus 'Leaving the black weed cover off means the rain, snow, wind will drain the soil of its natural goodness and therefore have poor soil in spring'.

Personally, I do whichever I feel is the easier, so no covering for me. However, this year I have dug over one side of my greenhouse and covered it with black plastic because I need the soil as warm as possible as I have ordered some sweet potato slips. £12 for eight slips: it *is* expensive and I could buy a sack of sweet pots for that, but I want to see if I can grow them. I did try to grow them from sweet potatoes bought from the supermarket but they died before they could sprout slips.

The Cowboys

I walked over to The Cowboys' plot, hoping they were working on it. They had two plots between the three of them; they
hadn't had them long, seemed a nice crew and seemed very
keen. They had just finished putting their shed up, and against
the fence leaned a greenhouse waiting to be erected. I was especially pleased that these had gone to The Cowboys as I had
found them in the advertising section of the supermarket:
'FREE but must dismantle and remove'. John Farthing and his
son went for them and brought them here and they were sold
on to The Cowboys for £25 each. They deserved them, you
could see the amount of work gone into the plots in readiness
for spring: the two plots had been dug over, beds sectioned off,
paths made. The area for the greenhouse had been prepared.
Fruit trees were already in place. They had done well.

The three of them were half bothers (not sure you can have
three halves), Wayne, Shane and Roy. It was Roy who first
made the joke about their mum liking the cowies. Since then,
they have been referred to as "The Cowboys".

You could see they were brothers, but all very different. Wayne was the eldest and wouldn't look out of place in the front line of the All Blacks: a big six-footer, dark complexion, mass of curly black hair, broad face and big smile. He laughed easily and was ready to help anyone.

Shane too was over six foot, similar build but with a shock of sandy hair and freckles: he looked like he would feel at home in a tartan kilt as a member of a long-ago Scottish clan. He was a surly, angry young man, hesitant to join in, although I have not spoken to him more than 'hello' and 'doing well'. You could feel the anger emanating from him, that at any moment he could blow; it was easier just to keep your distance from him. Both these men looked like they had very physical jobs, moving mountains around or pulling up trees without the aid of machinery.

Roy (named after the legendary Roy Rogers, we all assumed) must have been conceived in their mum's arty period. The youngest, at about twenty-two, Roy was slightly different: tall, fine-boned, shoulder-length brown hair tied back, pale complexion, with a boyish attitude to life. Roy was still at college studying fine art and it was Roy who I was hoping to see today. Unlike his brothers, I doubted Roy could pull the skin off a rice pudding but it wasn't pudding-skinning skills I was after, it was his computer skills. I needed advice, but no one was to be seen.

I started to walk back to my plot when I heard a commotion coming from the shed. I could see the shed start to rock from side to side, hear objects being smashed. I could also hear Shane shouting at the top of his voice, 'You cheating bastard!' and Wayne's voice getting angry, saying, 'Knock it off, Shane, stop NOW . . . I told you to knock it off!' then the shed door flew open. The back of Shane appeared, his feet dangling, his hands grabbing the shed doorframe with no success, then with one huge push he ended up sitting in a freshly dug and manured bed. Wayne stood over him, daring him to try and move. Roy was doubled over and leaning against the shed door, clutching his stomach. Shane thought the better of trying to commence battle and sat for a moment, then said, 'But we agreed it was £50 between us, now the cheating bastard is asking for another 100 quid.'

Wayne bent down and helped his brother up, saying, 'Just calm down, Shane, or we will be thrown off before we have started and mum will kill us.' Then, helping him up, he said, 'Come on, let's sit down and work out what has happened.' Shane sneered at his younger brother, still holding his stomach.

Roy moved back to make sure he was not in reaching distance as Wayne pushed his brother back in the shed. As he went to close the door, he noticed me standing at their gate; I must have looked horrified. He looked back at the two brothers and didn't speak to them, but they didn't move as Wayne walked to the gate. I thought of making a quick retreat but Wayne was an open person with a big heart and easy to read and there was no aggression there. He looked sad, upset and embarrassed. He put his massive hands on the gate, looked at me then at the ground, and said, 'I have to stop him from knocking lumps out of Roy all the time, it's a daily occurrence in our house these days. It's down to me to control him. Sorry if we gave you a fright.' I smiled and told him I had four brothers who were always fighting; mind you, they were not as big as his. As if talking to himself, he said, 'Sometimes when Shane loses it, I worry what will happen if I'm not there.' My motherly instincts took over and I patted his arm and said I was sure Roy could look after himself.

'It's not him I'm worried about . . . sorry again!'

He walked back up the path to the shed and closed the door behind him. I had forgotten what I had gone for.

Picking the Girls Up

Sunday was the designated day; a quiet day on the roads, we could take our time and have a nice drive into the Lancashire countryside, visit some farms, view some hens and have a lazy pub lunch. The main aim of the day was to visit three farms that were "disposing" of hens that had gone past their laying best. We were going to inspect the girls and make a decision on which we would give a home to. It wasn't going to be an easy decision as they all had so many to dispose of, and we only wanted six. We could at a push accommodate eight but we didn't want to overcrowd the girls, so six it was. We decided that we would go to the furthest farm first then we would look for a pub and visit the other two farms on the way back, making notes about each. When we got home we would compare notes and decide on which ones to buy. We toyed with buying two from each farm to keep it fair.

We needed to do some final jobs on the coop (it still needed one side making fox-proof) during the week then phone one or even three lucky farmers to organise picking the girls up the following week. Simple.

I picked Kitty up at 10 am on Sunday morning as agreed. The weather was a bit cloudy but said to improve by lunchtime. We set off with an air of excitement; we were going out for the day in the countryside and having lunch at a homely country inn so we both took the opportunity to dress up accordingly— in our Sunday finery.

I watched Kitty as she came down her path. She always reminded me of the swinging sixties in a long, flowing, tiered, hippy-type skirt and open-toed sandals. Her uncontrollable red hair as usual was tied up in a scarf but managing to flow over her shoulders. She suited the style and looked lovely, every bit a spring outfit. I wore long, navy blue trousers, a pale blue double-breasted jacket with gold buttons, and a pair of modest heels. We put our jackets on the back seat, and with sunglasses at the ready and map in hand, we set off. The first farm, Haven Farm, was just thirty-five miles away: a quick drive down the M6 onto the M65 to Upper Riley, turn left at the roundabout and Haven Farm was one mile down the lane. There was sure to be a nice little country inn between Upper Riley and our next farm. Easy peasy.

The M6 was busy but we were moving well by the time we turned onto the M65; it had started to rain a little but we weren't deterred. We carried on looking for signs for Upper Riley or the A657. After about twenty minutes, we saw a sign for Riley and decided that it must be close to Upper Riley and came off, following signs for Riley. It was still raining and visibility was getting worse. It was now near 11.30 am. We travelled down an A-road for two miles until we came to a roundabout pointing left for Riley. We passed through Lower Riley, Riley Downs, neither of which had any visible buildings, Little Riley, which consisted of a shop with a post box and two houses, then came Riley Bottom which was a post office, Spar and a pub called The Bottom Inn. The name "Riley" was big in these parts and they used it liberally. It was near 12 noon and the rain had stopped, thankfully. The Bottom Inn was advertising a roast turkey dinner stating "locally grown turkey". We decided that as soon as we had found out where we were and where we were going, a turkey roast was just the thing on such a cold, wet day.

We asked at the Spar for the way to Haven Farm. The Asian assistant, with little to no English, called the manager as they had never heard of it—nor had the manager. We showed the manager our map, with Kitty telling him that we were en route to buy some rescue hens for our allotment. He looked at the map and pointed to where we were, a good twenty miles out, but suggested that we take a look at the local farm which was having a few problems at the minute—it had loads of hens it wanted to get rid of.

Twenty miles out was something of a shock, but at least we could see some hens. Maybe not the ones we intended but still, we would go with it. We decided to see these and return to The Bottom Inn for a lovely locally grown roast turkey dinner. The manager wrote the directions down for us and we set off. It was only five minutes' drive away and he had told us to drive up the long, winding path to the farmhouse and once we were there to just hoot our horn and the farmer would come out.

It had started to rain again. We followed the map to the letter. As we came upon the entrance to the farm, there was a large sign announcing "Free Range Eggs, Farm Reared Turkeys". Feeling pleased with ourselves after our last mistake, we turned into a long, narrowing lane, flanked on both sides with overgrown hawthorn scratching the side of my car. Suddenly, we ended up in a large farmyard where we stopped and looked ahead at an ivy-covered, unkempt farmhouse. There was a dimly-lit room upstairs, smoke was bellowing out of the tall chimney. Feeling nervous at the sight of the eerie old house, I wound the window down to see the yard more clearly as the thought of just turning and leaving now seemed a sensible option. Kitty looked at me and said, 'Dear God, what's that smell?'

'It must be that chimney. I'll turn the car round and if no one has arrived by then we will go.' Kitty just nodded. I looked around to see how I could turn around. The stench of something burning was overpowering. I rolled the window back up quickly. To the right of the house was a large, old, wooden barn with big double doors, like something you would see in a Western movie. Next to that was a long, flat, concrete building with a heavy metal door; there was another smaller version set to the right, again with a metal door. No windows and both had security cameras on the corners. Next to this was a large metal container with a lid; there was a skip to the side of the metal container. The area around was unkempt and muddy. There was a faint droning noise coming from the buildings.

To the left of the house was a large carport-type building; it housed a very large horsebox in beautiful condition, only about two years old. We could see beyond the carport to what looked like stables. I looked at Kitty and, without a word, we agreed on a quick exit. It was pouring down. I revved the car to start turning but before I could move, four large German Shepherds came barking and jumping at the car. We both froze. Kitty screamed and shouted, 'Jesus Christ, let's get out of this place!' However, to do that I would have to move forward to do a U-turn in the farmyard, and as much as the dogs scared the life out of me—they were still jumping and circling the car— I couldn't harm them. Kitty was getting very anxious when a voice shouted, 'Down, now!' The dogs instantly laid down where they were.

I could feel myself getting very hot and sweaty. The house door was open and an old man came out wearing long, brown overalls, large glasses and a flat cap; he was short and a bit unsteady on his feet: he reminded me of Ronnie Corbett. He bellowed, 'Back!' and pointed behind him. The dogs obeyed and retreated behind him. I took a deep breath and rolled the window down again as he approached. I looked at Kitty and she was the same colour as Sugar—boiled shite.

'Are you from the Spar?'

'Erh, no. Linford. We were looking for Riley?'

'Who? Sam from the Spar rang and said you were on your way. Want some hens, he said. Follow me.'

He started to walk towards the big wooden barn with the dogs following him, wagging their tails. We got out and followed as obediently as the dogs. We kept looking at each other thinking we should run for it while we could. Instead we followed Ronnie. As we approached the large double doors I could feel my feet squelching and my pants dragging in the mud.

He turned and said, 'When I open this door, don't hang about, just run in fast or they'll all be out fast as sh . . . muck off a shovel . . . okay? Come closer!'

We both nodded and shuffled towards him. He turned to the dogs and bawled, 'Stay!' We were wringing wet, cold and frightened but did as we were told. He pushed one of the doors and it moved in various directions: the top stayed put, the bottom moved inwards, the dogs shifted nearer.

'Ready?'

The dogs moved even closer, pressing against my legs. I could feel the heat from their bodies and their anticipation. I began to feel sick and I looked at Kitty, her eyes wide, looking at me. I could read her thoughts: *what the hell are we doing?*. He pushed the door again and it gave a few inches, then he shoved us in. For a fraction of a second, a shaft of light shone down the barn, revealing a mass of brown heads and feathers. For a nanosecond, the hens looked still and surprised, then made an almighty rush for the door, squawking at the top of their voices. The dogs began to bark and bounce around, trying to get in. The door shut behind us with an almighty *bang*; everything was dark and quiet except for a slight shuffle next to us. Ronnie started to move.

'Out the bloody way, move!'

The dogs started to whimper outside. It was pitch black, you could hear the hens moving but not making a sound. What possessed us to follow a strange man into big old barn now guarded by four German Shepherd dogs, I don't know! We could hear Ronnie stumbling over things and moving things around and then a neon light flickered on and we could see a massive barn full of grown hens perching on bars, pallets, hay everywhere. On the left was a tall, rusty metal machine covered in dust and feathers; it appeared to be attached to a conveyer belt at the far end. The sweat was pouring down my back—or was it rain? Kitty looked terrified.

There were eggs everywhere: on the machine, lying on the floor, broken ones, shells, boxes, everything was smelly and dirty. The dogs were whimpering and whining, desperate to get in. We could see noses under the door and hear the scratching as they were trying to dig their way in. I had hold of Kitty's hand; she squeezed mine so hard I wanted to shout out. Near the machine stood six wooden pallets, each with trays and trays of eggs standing about five feet high.

'D'ya know anything about computers?'

We just shook our heads.

'Bastard! I can't work it out, it just stopped and I don't know what to do. That Currie woman! All these eggs, no use, all condemned, can't sell any of them, and the bloody hens still laying like mad. My son-in-law said he would look at it but he is so busy with the turkeys,' he said, shaking his head from side to side. 'All these eggs wasted. This machine, this bastard cost thousands and I have had no end of problems. I'm sure her husband owns the egg machine company!'

'Why?'

'I told you, the bloody computer is broken.'

We just stood looking at him blankly, then from nowhere Kitty, in an effort to pacify him, muttered, 'Can we buy some of the eggs?'

'No, they are not for sale.'

'Why?'

'Because the computer is broken.'

'What has that got to do with it?'

He looked at Kitty like she was from another planet. 'I can't stamp them, I can't sell them, I can't give them away, all I can do is destroy them. What do you do with this many eggs? And it's growing daily.'

'Why?'

'Why?' He was becoming irate. 'Because I told you, the bloody computer is broken and the computer works the machine, the machine that separates them into size, then stamps them and feeds them onto the trays. No computer, no nothing. How many do you want?'

Looking at me for approval, Kitty said, 'Eight dozen, please. Have you tried turning it off?'

Again, looking at Kitty like she had special needs, 'You will never get ninety-six in that car. You'll need a trailer.'

'I meant eggs. Have you tried turning it off and then on?'

Looking from Kitty to me, he shook his head. 'There is a chance it will work when it's on, and there's definitely no chance it will work when it's off.'

Kitty let go of my hand, shuffled through the straw and chick poo and walked to the computer.

'Have you checked all the cables?'

He again looked at me, but now he was thinking maybe she wasn't so daft. 'No, it just went off.' He was pressing the return key on the computer repeatedly. 'The eggs were flying everywhere,' pointing at the mountain of eggs broken on the floor, the ones backed up on the machine and the ones he had stacked.

As though she was talking to a naughty child, Kitty said, 'Let's turn the computer off, unplug everything, check all the cables are connected properly and then we can turn it on again and see what happens.'

Ronnie just looked and muttered, 'Yeh, let's . . . suppose anything is worth a try, I suppose.'

Kitty turned the computer off, unplugged it from the mains, and together they went over each section of the machine, making sure that it was completely unplugged, then they set about checking all the cables and connections. Hens kept trying to get involved, squawking when Ronnie would just bat them away. Some came up to me, just staring at me. I'm sure they were pleading for me to open the door.

After a few minutes, Kitty crawled from under the conveyer belt, completely absorbed in what she was attempting to do and not noticing that her Sunday best skirt was covered in hen poo, her knees were black from the filthy floor, the hem was wet and muddy, and her scarf had shifted sideways. Underneath the hen muck on her face, the colour seemed to be returning.

'Have you got any instructions on the computer, you know, when you first got it?'

Ronnie scrabbled round the desk drawer and came out with a sheet of A4. Together they read through the steps and plugged the computer and the machines back in. They went through the order in which they should be turned on. The machine first, then the stamper. It made various waking-up type noises which was promising, I hoped. Then the computer: Kitty read the starting up details and implemented them slowly. When they came to the last part, they looked at each other and Ronnie crossed his fingers and Kitty did the same. Kitty pressed the start instruction and the whole thing came alive, making a terrible din. The hens ran to the back of the barn in fright. The back belt was running, the smaller front one was going, the funnel things were moving. It worked—Ronnie was ecstatic. He went to hug Kitty but thought better of it.

He explained how it all works: the eggs go on the back belt and are sorted into size by these funnels, then they are fed down onto these trays on the front belt which takes them under the stamp machine which dates them. 'I take them off there and stacked on the pallets ready for sale but, thanks to Mrs Currie, if they're not stamped I can't sell them.'

Ronnie was clearly delighted. 'Wait until John sees this. He said he would fix it but God knows when that was going to be! Thank you, thank you so much!' He looked at me with a "she's not so dim" look.

'Hens, how many do you want?'

We tried to explain we were just looking really and intended to come back when we made a decision. Plainly he didn't hear us.

'My girls give you loads of double yolkers, have you got a box?'

'No, we didn't intend—'

'Never mind, we'll just put them in the boot.'

'The boot? No, we don't want them shut up in the boot.'

He looked wide-eyed at us, again with the mystified look!

'Okay, wait here,' and he disappeared out the door, giving it a hefty shove closed, shouting, 'Stay!' at the dogs as he passed them.

We stood looking at each other. 'What now?' Kitty said.

'How did you do that with the machine?'

'It's the same with my computer, sometimes you just have to turn it off, give it time to think about the error of its ways and start up again. Doesn't always work but it did today. Either that or one of the cables had come loose, and given the number of hens sitting on it, that was probably it.'

The door was forced open by two cardboard boxes, followed by Ronnie. 'Grab these,' he said before shouting, 'Stay!' to the dogs. He put his shoulder against the door to shut it and said, 'Right, how many do you want?'

It was too late to argue. 'We thought four would be plenty for now. How much are they?'

'Any particular ones take your fancy? They are about twelve months old and will lay well enough for you. I wanted to get rid of them because of the egg machine. I will have to dispose of all these eggs but at least I'll be able to start up again. Now a word of advice: soon as you get these home, clip their wings or they'll think they can fly!'

Kitty pointed to the nearest and I picked one that was nearly bald, obviously hen pecked. Ronnie bent down and scooped them up by their feet and dropped the four headfirst into a box. We immediately delved into the box in an effort to upend the poor chickens but they didn't need any help and as soon as they were upright they were trying to escape.

'Shut the box or they'll be out, quick!'

Kitty quickly put her foot on the box which was squawking and rocking from side to side, little heads trying to pop out.

'I need the other one for standing!' said Kitty, laughing and looking at me as I raised my feathered, hen poo covered, heeled shoe and placed it on the top of the rocking box.

Ronnie was standing ready to open the door. 'Right, when I open the door, don't fanny about.' He stood watching as Kitty and I tried to pick up a moving box each and at the same time keep the lids closed. He eventually left the door and came over to help. 'Right, I will take them one at a time. You come with me and open the boot . . .'

Kitty was mortified. 'We can't put them in the boot!'

'Why not?'

'Well, it's just not, not, ethical, locking pets in the boot!'

'They're hens!'

'We can't put them in the boot, they can go on the back seat.'

'Up to you but you'll have hen muck everywhere. Okay. Ready? Let's out and close the door bloody fast or they'll be away.' They knew we were about to open the door, they were on the starting blocks, waiting for the starter gun.

I shuffled my box of hens to the door, placed my foot back on the lid and pulled opened the door just enough to let them out. The dogs were excited and started to bark and bounce up and down; one managed to get his nose caught in the door. I heard a terrible yelp as I shoved my back against the door to close it as fast as I could. The starter gun had gone off, hens were descending on me, hundreds of them with their funny little sideways run skidded into me and the door, knocking me sideways, off my one leg onto the floor. The box fell open and the four hens joined the melee and disappeared into the tide of brown feathers.

I could hear the dogs barking as they followed Ronnie and Kitty to the car. I managed to sit up, dazed and winded; the race was over, the hens had retreated. The box was empty, the hens had escaped back into the hoard. Was that attack a ploy just to save their fellow hens? It had worked. My hands were covered in muck, feathers, straw, egg and all the rest that was on the floor of the barn. I turned onto my knees and stumbled upwards with the help of the door.

I heard the car door shut and the dogs approaching, followed by a knock at the door, Ronnie shouting, 'Are you ready? We are going to open the door. Stand back!'
I moved away and once again could see the hens waiting to start, and whimpered, 'Okay.' Ronnie was well practised with the door and they were both in in a flash. The hens hardly moved. They both looked at me. Kitty laughed and said, 'What happened to you? They rescued their mates.'

Ronnie grabbed another four hens by their feet and upturned them, telling Kitty to bring the box. I was told to open the door, go through it, let the two of them out and pull it closed *fast*. I was glad to be leaving.

The Turkeys

The rain eased off long enough for us to get to the car. The
dogs played around the yard, now quite bored of us. Ronnie
put the box on the floor, dropped the squawking hens in and
closed the lid, then lifted them onto the back seat of the car.
We weren't prepared for hen transit today so we searched in
the boot for a weight to put on top of the boxes to keep them
secure as we drove home. Ronnie assured us that once they
were in a darkened place they would be calm and quiet. All we
could find was a large sheet of folded black plastic which we
put loosely over the top of the boxes. We then threw our jackets on top of the plastic. They quietened down immediately.

We tried to pay Ronnie but he was so pleased about the computer he wouldn't accept anything. He explained that it was his
family farm that kept cattle, pigs and sheep, but he was getting
on, and when his only child, a daughter, had married a local
farm boy he handed the family farm to her and her husband to
run. He ran the egg sales for pin money but his son-in-law ran
the farming business now and was into modern methods of intensive farming. By the look on his face, Ronnie disapproved
of it (and his son-in-law).

He pointed to the concrete buildings. 'See those? He built them to breed the turkeys in. He buys them in as day-old poults and keeps them in there, in near darkness, overfeeds them and they never see the outside, never breed. They don't even have enough room to walk around. They are kept for about three months, then taken into that other building where they are stunned before being slaughtered, plucked and cleaned ready for sale . . . breeds thousands a year. As one lot goes out, the place is cleaned and another lot arrive within twenty-four hours. He has the nerve to call them home-reared fresh turkeys . . . my backside. I call it intensive farming! They never see the outside, never breed, don't have enough room to walk around. That's not what I call farming!'

'Why are they kept in the dark?'

'Evidently, it makes them less aggressive, but if I was kept in a concrete building with no room to move, overfed and never let out, I would be aggressive. When they are killed, all the "other" bits are either sold for pet food or burned—hence the pong!'

Suddenly, the dogs jumped to life and headed for the path, barking and bouncing around. A horse and rider came trotting up the path. The horse was a lovely looking animal, chestnut brown with a white face; the rider, a pretty young lady covered in mud but smiling happily. She trotted up to us. 'Hi, Dad. I am wet through, but a good run. Barney enjoyed it. Hello.'

She was the apple of his eye as he beamed at her.

We just stood looking at her and her horse; even plebs like us could see it was a thoroughbred and a lovely animal.

Kitty admired it and asked if it raced.

'Point-to-point.'

'Is he any good?' The horse snorted as if showing his annoyance at someone questioning his ability.

'Won the Essex Cup last year,' she said, patting the side of his neck.

We had no idea what she was taking about!

Ronnie interjected. 'Worth a fortune, aren't you?' rubbing Barney's nose. 'These ladies have fixed the egg machine.'

'Oh good. Better get him rubbed down and fed. Bye.'

She was neither interested nor impressed by the news. The beautiful rider and the beautiful horse trotted off with the dogs running around their feet and made their way to the stables behind the carport.

We made our goodbyes and thanked Ronnie again for the girls, but he was still thanking Kitty for fixing 'that bastard' as we left. Through the rear window, I could see the girl dismounting. More horses' heads popped out of the nearby stables to greet them and a flurry of activity began.

Kitty said, 'Spoilt cow. If I get the opportunity to come back in another life as an animal, I don't want to come back as a chicken . . . or a turkey . . . *especially* not a turkey! Maybe a horse. I'll have to find out a bit more about point-to-point before I make the decision.'

'So *that* is locally bred turkeys.'

The Road Home

We drove slowly down the path towards the main road. The weather was starting to brighten up and we were glad to be on our way home, and pleased that Ronnie Corbett turned out to be quite a nice bloke and not the mad axeman we had originally thought.

At the bottom of the farm path, I stopped and checked my face in the mirror. I looked at my reflection then looked at Kitty. It was a toss-up for who looked the worse. Her scarf had slid sideways and she was filthy dirty. We just looked at each other. Kitty hitched her skirt up to reveal her sandals and hem of her skirt. My lovely blue jacket was filthy, my feet were wet and my shoes were covered in chicken poo, and I was sure my disaster in the barn meant I was sitting in the same. I looked at the time on the car clock: 1.30 pm.

'Do we want a turkey roast dinner?' I asked.

'You mean *locally* bred turkey?'

'Don't think I will ever eat turkey again!'

'Don't think they would let us in anyway, looking like this.'

'Which way do we go?'

'God knows! But best make a start. At best it will take about two hours.'

We started to laugh. Kitty said she thought we were done for when we went in that barn. I said it was like a Hitchcock movie and was waiting for the music to start. I wish I had taken a photo of you on all fours, in your best skirt under a conveyer belt with the chickens all around you. We laughed until the tears ran, making clean streaks down our faces. We made the decision to turn right and hope for the best: just head for the M6 then to the allotment.

It took us a few more lanes before we found an A-road. We laughed about our ambitions for the day and how badly it had gone. After a few miles and no road signs, we stopped and asked a pedestrian for directions to the motorway. He bent down and approached the car, but as Kitty lowered the window he quickly withdrew and just pointed, saying, 'Down there, about two miles.'

As we drove off, Kitty shouted, 'Thanks! What's up with him?' We drove on for another couple of miles before we eventually joined a very busy motorway with huge semi-trailers travelling too close to the vehicles in front, beeping their horns if they were in any way put out. We settled into the slow lane and felt relieved to be on our way home.

Kitty and I chatted away, sympathising with the turkeys and the chickens all being locked up and then slaughtered. We were filtered from three lanes into two as we passed by a roadworks sign saying 'ROADWORKS 15 MILES. NO HARD SHOULDER. SPEED LIMIT 50'. Traffic was moving at quite a speed, and in order to filter into the moving traffic I had to speed up quickly, move into the new lane and then hit the brakes as the car in front hit his. This caused the boxes in the back to jerk forward and sideways, moving the plastic sheeting and the coats holding the lids down on one of the boxes. I checked them in the rear-view mirror—all seemed ok. The motorway was busy and took all my concentration. Then one head appeared out of the box, then two more. At first, they just looked round, but then, as the traffic passed at great speed, they began to squawk. We could hear the wings flapping against the box as they were trying to escape. I was mortified but kept my concentration on the driving. I shouted to Kitty but she had already turned and stretched back, trying to shove their heads back in the box which sent them into a mega panic. She grabbed the coat from the other box and threw it over their heads, pushing them back in, and collapsed back into the seat with a sigh of relief. We began to laugh that sort of hysterical laugh when you feel disaster has just been averted.

The traffic had slowed to a crawl. I was concentrating on driving when, out of the corner of my eye, I could see two kids in the car next to us were laughing and pointing to us.

The removal of the coat left the second box without sufficient weight to keep the chickens in, but we were so busy wondering why the kids were laughing (and laughing with them) and what was so amusing, we hadn't noticed. One scheming chicken never made a sound until she was sitting on the back window. She'd squatted, and as soon as I saw her, she squawked her head off. Her fellow captives were out in a flash, wings flapping and trying to join her. The cars beside us were enthralled and having fits of laughter, until the realisation of the situation hit them: they either hit the brakes or the accelerator, whichever they found most appropriate. Behind us was a large semi-trailer whose driver was driving far too close but was enjoying the show. The first escapee played to the audience, squawking and strutting from side to side.

Kitty took off her seatbelt, turned around and tried to climb into the back. She got her left leg and upper body through the seats but her skirt was caught on the seatbelt. She pulled at it and then tried to lift her right leg over the seat, not realising in her panic—she was now the star of the show. She was virtually upside down and her skirt had been pulled down around her thighs, showing her knickers to the other cars and the semi driver. Stretching as far as she was able in an effort to catch the chickens on the back window, her left leg was in the back but her right was stuck across the top of the passenger seat. She gave another tug on the skirt and it ripped apart, then fell into the back seat knocking the second box of chickens. The two escapees were now joined by the other three. The semi-trailer man was in hysterics, slapping the wheels and rolling around laughing—he was far too close. The first escapee was still squawking and the others were joining in, most of them happy just to sit on the back window, but not all. Some decided to test their flying skills and launched themselves at the front of the car. They didn't care about the car upholstery or the fact I had given it a good clean for this very expedition. They deposited their manure anywhere the urge came over them. Nor did it occur to them the danger they were putting us all in.

The more upset they became, the more deposits arrived. The stench was terrible. Suddenly, the automatic window on the passenger side started to open. Kitty screamed, 'Don't! They'll be all over the motorway!' One of the flying chickens had landed on the automatic window button situated between the seats. I could feel the perspiration running down my back, panic was setting in. I managed to shoo the hens away and close the window before any escaped.

Kitty was half on the back seat and half on the floor, managing at all times to keep her backside in the air. The semi-trailer man had his phone out and was trying to video the action in our car. More signs: 'PLEASE KEEP IN LANES'! Cars were travelling alongside us, pointing and laughing before escaping a potential accident. Kitty righted herself and started again, trying to catch them and put them in the box, throwing the coats over the lids. She was successful with three but the other three just squawked, looking out the window at the traffic, then, in fright, flapped their wings, trying to fly around the car and launching themselves on the front windscreen. I was trying to bat them away with one hand and trying to drive in a straight line. It was pandemonium. As soon as Kitty caught one it would flap and peck at her. She swore profusely as she tried to put it in back in the box, then the others were trying to escape. The first one was still on the back window, strutting and squawking at full pelt. All that sympathy for the poor locked-up chickens had well gone. I could have strangled all of them, starting with the ringleader on the back window.

I shouted at Kitty, 'We will be back on the main highway soon and be able to pull over. Stop chasing them, maybe they will keep still for a few minutes.' Half-lying across the boxes with one arm, her other over my shoulder in an effort to protect me from flying chickens, we carried on until the two lanes went to three and the hard shoulder appeared. As I pulled onto it, the semi-trailer man passed us at speed and honked his horn, sending the chickens into a flying frenzy again. I shouted abuse at him and could have strangled him too.

I turned off the engine. We waited until we had all calmed down. Together we caught the two fliers, then the ringleader who was now just perched on the back window, looking as innocent as a new born. Kitty grabbed her, unsympathetically, and plunged her into the box. When we had them boxed up, Kitty put what was left of her skirt on. She tried to push her scarf back in position and, with deep breaths, we calmed ourselves once more, then threw all the coats on top of the boxes before opening the car doors. The gusts from the passing roaring traffic nearly blew me off my feet; the noise was frightening all of us and the chickens complained loudly. The urge to commit chicken murder was hard to suppress.

We shoved the boxes in the boot, slamming the lid down with more force than necessary. We got back into the car in silence. Mild hysteria and relief were taking over now. Kitty started first with:

'I could easily murder them hens!'

'If you murdered a hen, would it be henicide?'

'What?' looking at me like I was a complete lunatic.

'Would it be called henicide or chickicide? If you murder your parent it's called patricide and if you kill yourself it's called—'

'A very bad day!'

'Suicide. So if you kill a hen or chicken is it—'

'Cockicide?'

'That bloody semi-trailer bloke needs cockiciding, he was taking a video of it all.'

'Oh my God, if it goes on YouTube, it'll be on Facebook. Oh my God!'

'No one will know it's you—he could only see your knickers!'

Hysterical laughter took over.

We calmed ourselves and I started the engine up. Checking the rear-view mirror, I began to move forward. I turned the engine off, got out of the car, fending off the rain and the blustering wind again, went into the back and returned, slamming the door and giving Kitty the deposit-covered egg.

Kitty smiled sweetly. 'Ooh, our first egg, how lovely,' then opened the window and threw it in the bushes. She closed the window and smiled. 'That's eggicide!'

We were exhausted and stressed and once again laughed with that manic hysteria brought on by fright.

We set off once more. The rain had started again, it was 2.30 pm and at this rate we wouldn't get back before it went dark, and the coop wasn't fox-proof yet. The more we tried to travel faster, the slower we became. Mythical problems slowed the traffic down for mile after mile; we kept waiting to pass the accident or the breakdown but nothing eventuated. Then, without rhyme or reason, it would speed up, and with sighs of relief we would be off again only to be slowed down again by another mythical accident miles further on.

It took nearly four hours to get back to the allotment. It was pouring with rain and the last thing we wanted to do was go to the allotment and fix the coop. We toyed with the idea of visiting CRAPS but decided against it. We were tired and hungry and desperately wondering why we decided to get chickens, as up to now they have proven to be a real pain in the rear end.

It was nearly dark as we approached the allotment gates. An old timer was just closing them behind him but graciously reopened them and stood waiting for us to pass through. Kitty opened the window to thank him. The chickens were squawking away. He looked in the car and recoiled in horror. 'Jesus, what have you been eating?' Was there any point at this stage explaining? Kitty closed the window and we drove to my plot. It is probably true what they say: that you cannot smell your own stink. We knew there was a stench in the car—the pedestrian had given us a clue.

We had been desperate to get home and had become used to the stench. We even put the heating on as we were wet and cold, not to mention very dirty. But it must have left the old timer feeling nauseous.

We sat outside my plot; it was raining, blowing a gale, cold and getting dark. We had a boot full of noisy chickens that had been locked in there for hours without food and water and an incomplete coop that needed to be dealt with. We sat in silence for a few minutes, wondering how to tackle it.

'We can't see enough to fix the coop,' Kitty eventually said.

'What do we do?'

'Take them home with us?'

'Erh, *no!*'

'They may be dead for all we know!'

We listened to hear if they were still making a noise. Shame.

'What are we going to do?'

Another long silence, then Kitty suggested, 'Put them in my shed!'

This was the only realistic answer to our plight. We needed food, water and some bedding. We spent the next few minutes on mine and Kitty's plot in the rain and dark, coming up with some hay to put on the floor. I had kale still growing so we yanked a full plant up, nearly falling backwards in the effort. I threw the hay down first and then the kale. Kitty found an old biscuit tin and filled it with water. Still dressed in Sunday best, we tottered back to the car for the chickens. Taking them one box at a time, when both were safely in Kitty's shed, we opened the lids and withdrew quickly, closing the door behind us. Kitty secured the bolt with a lock and key, saying that it was just in case Sugar had been allowed out of hospital and came looking for a place to squat for the night.

Back in the car, we sat for a minute to catch breath. It was pouring and cold and we were very hungry. We backed down the lane and made our way to the exit gate. Kitty got out and opened it whilst I drove through. I drove Kitty home and we agreed that the following morning we would meet up at about 10 am, fix the coop and move the chickens in and all would be well with the world.

All the anticipated fun and excitement of the day had well and truly gone and the near hysteria had been replaced by tiredness, depression and starvation. Kitty got out of the car, saying how she hated the chickens. I watched her walk up her path; the automatic light flicked into action. Gone was the sixties hippy, gone was the scarf. The wild hair was showing its true capabilities and could have challenged a Worzel lookalike winner. She stopped at the door and took her sandals off, tossing them in the front garden. The lovely swinging sixties hippy look had gone and been replaced with a "Mad Margaret" lookalike.

As soon as I got home, I walked to the cupboard and poured a large glass of sherry and downed it in one. I then threw my clothes into the washing machine and prayed it didn't get clogged up. The shoes were beyond hope and went in the bin.

100

After a long bath, I was starving but too tired to cook. I needed something quick and easy; the only thing I could think of was eggs. I had a cheese sandwich and another glass of sherry, then another sherry, then started a letter to my lovely Megan.

The Next Day

I woke at 8 am the next day, so grateful for being home in my own bed and clean. It was a long time since I had slept past 6 am. It was raining still. I was in no hurry; the hens would be safe and dry, and quite soon they would have their nice new coop.

I opened the car door, trying to find the strength to clean the car. The stench nearly knocked me over. I knelt on the front seat to stretch and leaned over, putting my hand on the back of the passenger seat, and started to clean the poo bespattered dashboard. The smell was still nauseating: to think we sat in this for hours and didn't notice. It was everywhere, even the roof. I had put my hand in it and I was kneeling in it. I had to stop and take deep breaths of fresh air until I made myself dizzy. Even after I had taken the top layer of muck off, it still wreaked, but for now I would have to live with it until I could get it professionally cleaned. I went back inside and got several large towels and placed them over the seats.

I picked Kitty up on the way to the allotment and by the time we got to there it was gone 10 am. We set to getting the coop ready and transferring the hens. It would be true to say that the "shine" of having hens had completely gone. When we had finished and the hens were safely ensconced in their new home, I made a cup of tea and we sat in my shed, somewhat subdued, reviewing the previous day. Maybe one day we would look back and laugh, but unless the hens lay golden eggs we doubted it.

The weather was improving day by day and we both got busy in our allotments, forgetting the dreadful journey. The hens had settled in and after few days they began to lay. We did get a strange visit from the local council along with the RSPCA who had been informed that the chickens were not housed correctly, but they went away happy after giving the coop and us the once over.

Kitty and I raced to the plot each day to see if there were any eggs. We agreed to have turns in "egg checking" but most of the time we both turned up. We started to name them and referred to them as "the girls" after which we actually began to like them. They ran to the door of the run each day to meet us; they had funny little runs when they chased flies. They ate the weeds and best of all they laid lovely eggs. Some of the eggs were enormous; we tried to identify the girl who had laid such whoppers so we could rename her. We decided she would be the one with a startled look and would rename her "bright eyes". We were easily won over and within a week my car had been cleaned and it was all forgotten . . . well nearly!

After the excitement of the chickens, I wanted to make headway with my IT project and waited for The Cowboys to appear which took well over a week. As soon as I saw Roy and Wayne standing, hand on hips, discussing the greenhouse, I went over. Shane wasn't there, thank God. I shouted over the gate and they both came over to me and asked my opinion as to the best place to situate the greenhouse. They had reserved a place but now they'd looked at it, it was much bigger than John had told them. The place they had prepared was for a standard six by eight foot, but this was ten by eight foot. They were pleased about this, as everyone wants more greenhouse space. But it now left them with the problem of where to put it. After various options were explored, they decided to enlarge the original area and place it there.

I tried to explain to Roy my IT illiteracy problem and why it was important that I learned how to use Skype. He seemed keen to help, and when they finished with the greenhouse he would come over if I was still there and have a chat. I was delighted when, within the hour, he came purposefully striding up my path. 'Shane is on his way so I am keeping a low profile. So, what's the problem with the computer?'

I explained all about my lack of knowledge, that I wanted a computer as I would never be able to go to Australia to see my daughter and granddaughter. So contacting them via Skype seemed the most sensible thing to do but I didn't know what to buy or how to use it when I did. He laughed and said he helped his mum, and, 'If she can learn, anyone can.' Now she was quite good at using Facebook and emailing, so if he could teach her, he could teach me. He suggested he came to mine with his laptop to show me how it all worked and search for a cheap but fast laptop for me. I understood the relevance of cheap, but not fast. What did that mean? He would call in after college for an hour and see how we went. I gave him my address and telephone number. I began to get excited and wanted to tell Kitty; he seemed a genuine lad, easy to talk to and obviously could see me, so I wasn't invisible to him. As he stood to leave, he noticed the picture Megan had bought me. He took it down off the shed wall and went outside to study it further, saying it was very dirty, that it looked like it had been hung in a smoker's house. As we talked about the picture, Shane arrived. Roy quickly ducked back in the shed. He said Shane was not happy with the shed and greenhouse and thought that he was pulling a fast one on them. Before I could ask any more, Roy suggested that he took the picture to show his art teacher and see if it could be cleaned up. I tried to say it would cost a bit but he said it would be free as it would be part of a project he was doing. I stressed how important it was to me, that my granddaughter had bought it for me, that it was precious. He was insistent so reluctantly I agreed. Roy was watching Shane; as soon as Shane opened their gate and walked up the path, Roy darted out of my shed saying, 'Is 4 pm today okay?' I agreed and he left at speed.

Spot on time, Roy turned up at mine with a bag over his shoulder, which turned out to contain his laptop. After the first bout of nervousness based on 'I am too old to learn, I will never be able to learn at my age' had disappeared, I began to understand the fascination of computers, the internet, its powers of communication and I was hooked! Roy gave me instructions on contacting my telephone provider to ask about broadband, whatever that might be. My learning skills were seriously being tested, but if I can see and talk to my daughter and granddaughter, it would be worth the effort. When Roy left with his laptop, I suddenly felt quite alone. We agreed to meet again in a few days and we would start to search for a laptop and printer. I was so excited I could hardly wait but still didn't understand a word.

That night, I couldn't sleep and laid in bed watching the clock and trying to remember things Roy had shown me. But as emails, Facebook and Skype merged into one murky fog, I hoped somewhere in the near future I would be able to speak to and see my daughter and Megan—that's all I cared about. It must have been 3 am before I nodded off, full of hope and excitement.

The phone woke me about 8 am: some young man with a strange accent trying to convince me that I was entitled to PPI. It took him about three minutes to realise I was either stupid or still asleep and decided to just hang up. I got up and had a cup of tea and toast and made my way to the lotty by about 9 am. It was my turn to get there early and I was late. You have a sense of responsibility when you have chickens: you need to feed them, check the water, give the coop a bit of clean and, of course, collect the eggs before they decide to eat them or just squash them. For some reason we decided to go each morning; even though we left enough food and water for a week, we still went each day.

As I walked through the paths and past the metal plot that was now empty, I could smell smoke and wondered which shed had been burned down now. Fires happened mostly in the summer months when the kids were up late or the nightclubbers were looking for some excitement on their way home. Most plot holders accused Sugar, but as he was still in hospital, it was hardly likely to be him. As I turned into my lane, there was a small crowd gathering at my gate with John Farthing heading it up. My shed was still smouldering, the coop door was open and all the girls gone.

It must have happened in the early hours; no one saw, heard or knew anything. The pain returned. I leaned on the fence and practised breathing exercises I had seen on the telly.

The Fire

We all took to the lanes to look for the girls but we all knew by now that the foxes would have had them; we just hoped there may be one or two spared. None were found. My immediate thoughts were to give it all up. After Harry had worked so hard on the plot, and when he died, I kept it going for him. And now some unknown had come along in the middle of the night and destroyed it and released the girls—why bother? I went home saddened and miserable; it was Harry's shed and someone burned it down for no reason. At that moment, I thought I would never go back. I phoned Kitty and told her the bad news and she suggested, for the time being, we could share her shed until one came along for me. I told her I was devastated and would not be going back. All that work . . . the girls . . . Harry's shed—gone.

No one likes to think that they are disliked, but for someone to burn a shed and release harmless chickens, knowing their probable fate, smacked of more than dislike. The thought worried me and made me uneasy. The pain returned: probably stress and nerves but I will make an appointment to see the doctor.

I had forgotten Roy was coming until a knock on the door at the appointed time. He was there, laptop over shoulder and smiling. I was sure he could read my hesitancy but marched past me and opened the laptop up. Before I knew what we were doing, I was absorbed in the world of the information technology and the internet again. After an hour of searching, we agreed that the one I needed could be purchased online but, being a novice, I was reluctant to give my card details online to a total stranger from the Amazon, so we agreed that we would purchase it locally. Roy would set it up with the appropriate software (whatever that was). I thought I could just turn it on and it would work, like the toaster or the fridge, but no, it isn't enough to turn it on, you have to learn further stuff called software.

The following Saturday, I picked Roy up at his home. We were going to purchase my very own computer and printer. Roy lived in a small but neat terraced house close by. I couldn't help wondering how anyone brought three big lads up in what was obviously a two-up two-down. I knocked at the door and was invited in by his mum who introduced herself as Annie. (Maybe the cowboy theme ran through generations?) She was a short, slim lady with shoulder-length hair. The house was immaculate and gleamed like a new pin. Roy bounced down the stairs, smiling at me and saying, 'Come on, we have a computer to buy.' He went to kiss his mum on her cheek and she winced, so he stopped. That's when I noticed a fading bruise on the side of her face but well covered over with makeup.

Although Roy and Kitty told me this was possible and I understood the words they were using, somehow it just didn't sink in or I just didn't believe it. I was still apprehensive about Skype but I was feeling happier, thinking soon I may be able to speak to and see Megan and my daughter. But I wouldn't have been surprised if it did not happen as it sounded too good to be true.

It was 4 pm before we got back to mine. I made coffee as Roy unpacked it all and set it out on the front room dining table. With my £500 gone, I hoped it worked. We removed my boxes of antiques for the auctions and replaced them with cables, boxes, instructions, disks, polystyrene and cardboard everywhere. I began to wonder what I had spent my hard-earned savings on and if I would ever have a tidy house again. After about an hour, I was about to suggest Roy left it and came back tomorrow when suddenly he shouted, 'Eureka!' and the screen lit up and, more importantly, he had connected to the internet.

I was excited then. I wanted to know how to do Skype immediately. But no, there was more learning for me to do before we could Skype! Roy needed to set me up on email, with passwords, Facebook and Skype, then teach me how to use them.

Each time I felt Skype got closer, it faded into the distance.

Roy had to leave early as he had a big night out planned but would call in on Monday on his way home from college. As he left, I asked where—if he was going somewhere nice—and he said, 'To POPs.'
'Oh, going to see your dad?'
He laughed out loud, waving his hands around and said 'Dad? Oh God, no, I couldn't pick him out of a line up. No, POPs is on the High Street. I will be out all night if I'm lucky!'
I was trying to work out where he was going. There was a little church on the High Street, a "bush baptist" church as Harry used to call it. Must be that. The only other building was the old bank building that had been done into a wine bar but I had

never seen it open. 'What's a line up?' What were we talking about?

Roy left shouting, 'See you Monday!' I kept forgetting to ask about the picture; next time I would remember.

The phone rang and the familiar voice said, 'Is that you, Mrs L?' It was Kitty ringing me to tell me she had been watering my plants and they were okay but some were damaged as the person who did the deed trampled all over my newly-sown seedlings. Sugar was still in hospital with pneumonia and would be in for a while, so it wasn't him that burned my shed. I told her all about the computer purchase and how helpful Roy had been and about visiting Roy's house and the bruise. Kitty told me that the committee had arranged another meeting for a week this Sunday and asked if I was attending. I didn't have the heart for the allotment anymore but thought that the best thing would be to turn up and resign.

The following day was a long day. I kept looking at the computer and turning it on and off, just making myself at home with it. Each time the screen lit up it made a little noise, and each time I jumped. I read the manual until I realised I had no idea what I was looking at. Hurry up, Monday and Roy!

Monday came and went but no Roy. I didn't want to ring him as I didn't want to appear pushy. Wednesday came, still no Roy. I rang his phone, no answer. Thursday, Kitty rang to ensure that I was going to the meeting on Sunday; she would pick me up at 10.30 am. I brought her up to date with the Roy situation and asked if she had seen him on the plot. She said not, but Pretty Penny had been about with that "I know everything" smirk. I wrote my resignation and put it in an envelope addressed to the "The Chair". It had been a lonely week that started off with such promise, and now—no shed, no chickens and no Roy. I was concerned about Roy. It wasn't like him, or had I got him wrong? What was a "pop"? What has happened to the picture? Maybe it was a scam?

At 10.30 am on Sunday, resignation in hand, I would attend the meeting for the last time. When I got there, it was empty. I sat and waited a few minutes then my phone rang; it was Kitty saying she was at her shed and for me to go round as we had a problem. It was the last thing I needed. What was it, another fire? Maybe another break-in? But where was the committee? I didn't know what was going on so plodded round past the metal plot to Kitty's shed. Most of the committee was gathered there including The Cowboys, The Crims and Pretty Penny, but no sign of Mick.

114

There, on my plot, was a new shed. Not new as in shop new, but new to me. It was painted a bluey grey colour and had a little veranda with a trellis at the front, a hanging basket and a pot of flowers in the corner. I was speechless. Kitty ushered me up the path to the shed door and opened it with a 'tadaaaaaa . . .!' It had two big windows which where clad in pale grey gingham curtains; there were two chairs and a new mirror. It was lovely! I had to stop myself from crying. Above the door was a wooden sign "Marigold Hotel" written in italics and made by Roy.

Roy was clapping his hands in a childlike manner but he stopped immediately when he caught Shane standing head and shoulders above the rest of us, scowling at him. I could hear Pretty Penny complaining about the committee using society funds to buy sheds for 'their own'. Wayne, hearing the same, explained that they had found the shed by going on the free stuff site, and he, Roy and Shane took it down, transported it to the site and erected it. I would be asked to make a contribution to the society as everyone who gets a greenhouse or shed does. Kitty and The Crims had painted it and Roy had made the curtains. Penny was still droning on about the misuse of funds until I announced that I would be donating the going rate of £25 to the society for the shed and would reimburse people for paint, chairs and curtains. I was delighted and felt better than I had for a while.

The group started to drift away. As Roy started to leave, he said he was sorry he had let me down last week but was a bit busy, whilst smiling and nodding at the shed. Wayne teased him, saying if Roy had spoken to me he wouldn't have been able to keep his mouth shut! 'I know,' Roy giggled. 'See you tomorrow, same time same place?' I nodded in agreement and couldn't help giving them both a hug to thank them.

Life was improving again. A lovely shed, better than the one I had before. Roy was back on track and my lotty friends had proven to be real friends and pushed the boat out for me— especially Kitty. I was moved by it all and not even a little embarrassed.

When everyone had drifted away, Kitty went to her plot and brought back two cups of tea. We sat in my new shed and chatted for a while about plants, seeds, the bastards that had burned my shed, and how we needed to discuss the lottery syndicate as we had had no luck for ages. Kitty said The Crims would get us some more chickens if we wanted them. They had been really kind and wanted to help. Kitty and I talked at a normal level, but if the conversation touched on a delicate subject, heads moved together and voices lowered to a near whisper— as it did when we began talking about what a miserable pain Pretty Penny was and that no one had seen Mick for weeks, but Kitty had met him a couple of times "by accident" and he said he was too embarrassed now to show his face. She had even bumped into Pretty Penny in the supermarket and she told Kitty that Mick was lazy and had never worked, that she had to work to support them both. She even hinted that he was violent, stroking her face and saying she has learnt not to cross him. It was during this low frequency talk that the veranda squeaked. We stopped immediately and waited for someone to appear. Nothing. No one appeared. We carried on talking at a normal level about what we were going to grow and still we waited. No one appeared. Without stopping the chatter, we stood up and went to the shed door in time to see Pretty Penny disappearing out of the gate at speed. 'Oh God,' Kitty said, 'what did she hear?' I told Kitty that I would pay the going rate of £25 at the meeting on Sunday so all the world could see that I had paid. It was worth far more than £25, especially with all the work that had been done on it.

We discussed my improving IT skills, and as there was no chance of me being able to raise the airfare and the lottery was no good and the only possibility of being able to speak to and see Megan and my daughter was Skype, this was the most important thing for me at the moment.

Kitty had tried to get more information on the society being on the fiddle but no one was talking. We went over and over the buying and selling of sheds, the metal sales, everything was documented and receipts given so what else could there be? At least at this meeting the "fiddling" was top of the agenda.

SKYPE

As agreed, Roy came that Monday and suggested that we put a timescale on achieving Skype. We looked up the time difference in Queensland and agreed to meet after college and each night until Thursday, aiming to Skype on Saturday at approximately 11 am here which would be 8 pm there. We began setting up passwords which I had to write down and keep close but not let anyone else see or have them. I managed to send him an email which he returned using his phone. That's a step I can't see me ever doing. We practised sending emails as this was important when doing Skype.

I began to understand more. It is true that practice makes perfect, well, a lot better anyway, as I was practising sending emails, using a mouse, plugging and unplugging the router in case of problems—because at first just turning the computer on and off was a major step, now it is easy—, how it all linked up to the internet and basically how it all worked. In very simple terms, at times I felt confident, although this was often misplaced. Roy was a good teacher and when he realised I was getting stressed, he made me laugh. He'd say, 'In France, what we call Wi-Fi they call Wee-Fee, and in Spain, when we say 'www' they say 'oobly'!' He was a kind and understanding lad and I wondered how I could ever return his kindness.

I had written what turned out to be my last letter to Megan and my daughter asking for their email address, and from then on it was emails. Once I got a bit more confident, we organised a Skype session. I was so excited, I started to cry before I could see them. At first we just got their voices, then the pictures appeared: they were all sitting there looking at me and I was looking at them, seeing Megan live for the first time in years. She waved and said, 'Hi, Nana!' Roy found the box of tissues, stayed with me for a little whilst telling me not to touch anything, waved to my family and discreetly went to make us some tea.

We spoke for thirty minutes. Megan is a little adult now and so beautiful. When her mum and dad went into the kitchen to make tea, Megan put her face as close to the screen as she could and whispered something. I couldn't make it out; all I could do was say I didn't understand. Then she stood up and rubbed her tum and made a gesture as though she was pregnant. She couldn't be pregnant, she was only a child herself. My heart sank and I said, 'You're pregnant?' to which she giggled, 'No, not me,' and pointed to the kitchen. 'Shh, don't say anything, it's a secret. Don't say anything, Nan, or I am for the high jump!' Megan showed me her new dress and some shoes she was going to wear for a party this coming weekend. We discussed her school and her results in maths, her weakest subject. She explained a small maths problem which I managed to help her with, then she asked if she could contact me for help with her maths homework.

God knows where the answer came from, it was so far back I needed a pick axe to prise it out from my unused brain. I had gone through the box of tissues by the time we made arrangements to Skype again. Before we finished, Megan insisted on taking their laptop to her room to show me how cool it was. I was amazed to think you could just walk round with it and see the house. It was beyond belief. Megan's room was a typical girl's room: lots of pink, popstars on the walls, television, computer, stuff everywhere, and, of course, cuddly toys. I found it difficult to stop the tears; it was heaven. Megan wanted my mobile number so we could text each other. It was marvellous—every bit as good as I'd hoped. I just wanted to cuddle the computer with them in it. After about thirty minutes, we said our goodbyes and then they told me about the pregnancy. I acted suitably surprised and delighted. We made arrangements to speak again in a few days but I found it hard to say goodnight.

The pain returned quickly and more severely and I winced. Roy noticed and made me sit down. He asked if I had any aspirin, which I did, left over from Harry's medication, and told him where the medicine cupboard was. He went into the kitchen and came back with a cup of water and half an aspirin which I was told to let dissolve slowly under my tongue. He did first aid at uni, he said, and he was going to call an ambulance. I objected to this but promised to see the doctor first thing Monday. With reluctance, he suggested he made a cup of tea, but I insisted on a sherry. We chatted about my lovely family in Australia.

He had never known his dad, nor did any of his brothers know who their father was. He explained that his mum was a very kind person but a bit gullible, which hasn't served her well; but she was a good mum and they all loved her. Although Shane had a terrible temper and lashed out at anyone and everyone.

I thanked Roy for all his help with the new shed and really appreciated all he was doing for me. He was modest to a fault, saying everyone had a hand in it. I laughed and said, 'Even Pretty Penny?'

'God no, she was always around though to moan and complain.'

We discussed the opening of the shed and that I would ensure she saw the receipt for my £25 donation.

'Well, make sure she doesn't ask for more!'

The subject changed to his night out and I asked how it went. Evidently, he was home by 1 am, a pretty boring night by all accounts. I asked him what POPs was like and he started to laugh, then suddenly became serious. 'Never mention POPs to Shane. If he knew he would kill me.' In a low whisper, as though we were in a crowded room, he explained. I tried to keep the shock from my face as he told me he was gay and "Place of Pride" was a gay and tranny club. I should have guessed that he was gay. I tried to act worldly wise and all knowing. I wasn't completely sure what a "tranny" was.

'I take it that Shane doesn't approve?'

'To say the least. When he found the outfits he went mad—he went for me. Mum tried to stop him and that's how he gave her that black eye. It was an accident really, and it did stop him in his tracks because he was so sorry and upset and was more concerned with mum than me. When Wayne came home, there was World War Three. Me and mum ran out the house and didn't go back till midnight. You should have seen the state of the place: feathers everywhere, my sewing machine down the garden in a dozen bits along with the outfits, everything tipped over and broken.

Shane never usually gets a punch in, but this time Wayne had blood on his face so he must be improving. Wayne had managed to lock Shane up in his bedroom to let him cool down. That was a couple of weeks ago. Things are a bit calmer now, well at least in front of mum, but Shane is waiting for me and the shed money has given him the perfect excuse.'

'The shed money? What do you mean, the shed money?'

'Yes. He thinks I stole £100 and I didn't, I wouldn't. John Farthing asked for payment of £150, he said he and Shane agreed that as the shed and greenhouse were much bigger. They were £75 each so I took him at his word and gave him £150 from the pot, but Shane says it should have been £50 for them both and that I kept the £100 to fund my clothes.'

'Has he spoken to John Farthing?'

'Yes, and he showed Shane a copy of the receipt!'

'And?'

'It said £50 and it was signed. But it couldn't have been because he never gave me a receipt.'

124

It was later, as Roy was leaving, that I asked about the plumes and the outfits. The boyish child came out again and he flapped his hands around in the air. 'Well, its Pride Week in May and this year POPs are holding a carnival with twenty-five floats in a parade going through town. Everyone is entering and we were going to enter a dance float. I was making the outfits to wear. We really wanted to win as the winners go into the London Pride Carnival.' I was desperately trying to keep up with what he was saying and asked how he makes a float dance. 'No, it's dancers on the back of a float.'
'Oh, yes, I've seen them on the telly, very colourful. What type of dancers were you going as, ballroom or Latin American?' He dropped down on one knee, stretched his arm out and said, 'Tonight, Matthew, I'm going to be . . . a Tiller!'

Sometimes I think Roy is really, really clever with this knowledge of computers and then other times I think he is barking mad. I watched him walk down the path: he was tall, slim, elegant and fine-boned—he could easily be a Tiller Girl!

The Squirmers

I poured another sherry and sat at the table for a few minutes as it had been a very interesting evening. The pain and rapid heartbeat kept returning. I made a note to ring the doctors on Monday.

It was wonderful to see Megan and how she had grown and my lovely daughter was pregnant again. I longed to see them in real life again but realised it was never going to happen; I would have to accept Skype as a good second.

Roy and the shed money were dominating my thoughts. Was this the fiddle? How many people had we sold sheds and greenhouses too? How long had it been going on?

I turned the computer on and went to Google—how clever I felt. Me, Mrs L, an invisible old person, on Google. I wanted to ring someone up and tell them 'Look at me, I am on Google!' then it occurred to me I could go on Facebook . . . and tell everyone. I was painstakingly slow but got to the page Roy had set up for me. I put in Kitty's name and it came up, along with Kitty and lots of people I had never heard of, but lots I had. The magic of the internet had me again and before I knew it, it was midnight. But I had Facebook friends and I knew exactly what I wanted to do.

I didn't sleep very well, just lying there, waiting for morning so I could ring Kitty to ask her to give my apologies to the committee meeting as I was unwell, and ask that she paid my £25 for me and if she would ensure it went into the receipt book and if she could bring it to me so I could sign it. Also, when item number two came up on the agenda to explain that it was *my* item and to leave it until later as I was not to attend the meeting due to ill health.

Kitty asked lots of questions as to why I wasn't going, having said earlier that I would. I told her that I would explain every-thing later. At 12.30 pm, Kitty knocked at my door and we sat and discussed the meeting. The vicar was chair and he had a service at 12.30 pm so the meeting had started on time and fin-ished one hour later. He gave short shrift to anyone who dal-lied including John Farthing, who as normal complained bitter-ly about timewasters: 'There was absolutely no reason to put it on the agenda anyway, just causing trouble, stupid woman, and shouldn't be on the committee if she can't attend.' He was very reluctant to let the petty cash book out of his sight but the vicar, who was unusually brusque as he was in a hurry, took a quick vote on it and everyone but John agreed to let me have the book. The vicar asked for his concerns to be noted, to which the committee agreed, and promptly called the meeting to a close then left after ensuring John handed the receipt book over to Kitty.

I explained to Kitty about the conversation I had with Roy and how Shane was gunning for him over the cost of the shed, Shane throwing Roy's Tiller Girl outfits for the gay and tranny POPs pride parade, Shane giving his mum a black eye and how Wayne and Shane had a good set-to over it. Kitty interrupted me. 'No, no stop! Go back and start at the Tiller Girls and trannys, slowly, and let me catch up.' I repeated it again and about Shane speaking to John Farthing about the receipt for £25 signed by Roy, Roy insisting that he didn't sign a receipt, that he paid £150 for them both. Kitty's eyes refused to open any further as they were already at maximum. I went into the kitchen to make a cup of tea and let her think for a minute. When I returned with the tea, she was already in the petty cash receipt book.

The page for Roy had Roy's name signed on it for £50, so I looked—it was exactly as I thought. I couldn't help a little snigger to myself, sometimes you just knew you were right and this was one of those times. But first we had to prove it, and then, how would we deal with it?

I told Kitty my thoughts. If I was correct, any sales John had been involved in were probably fraudulent and the only way to prove it was to go through the book then contact the individuals concerned, asking them how much they were charged. This could be done discreetly and quickly with the use of my new best friend, Facebook.

We went through the petty cash book pages: there were fifteen sales, most of them last year, four this year. All paid £25 each according to the book. All were signed by the purchaser and countersigned by J. Farthing. We worked back in time, ignoring the last sale to Roy. Kitty knew two of the people and they were on Facebook. Kitty messaged them with a simple question, asking if they thought the shed or greenhouse was value for money as we were wondering whether to continue with the scheme. The first reply came more or less instantly, from Mrs Cook's mum and her daughter who had not long had their plot: 'The committee should be up front with the true charges and not mislead people' so we looked at each other and then checked the book again. Mrs P. Cook, plot A12, received £25, signed and dated and countersigned by J. Farthing. We went back to Mrs Cook and asked what she had paid. We knew what the answer was before it came. She was told it would be £25 but when it arrived she was asked for £75. We went back again and asked, had they signed for the shed and had they still got the receipt? The answer to both was 'yes', that she would scan it in and send within ten minutes so that we had a copy. Kitty asked her if she knew of any other plot holders that had purchased a shed or greenhouse. She told us about the man down the lane from her who had bought one, had had the same experience and thought the committee were on the fiddle. Mrs Cook only knew him as Ian but told us where his plot was: A18. The second man in the book, Mr Ian Evans, plot C29, took an hour to reply with a similar story and he had the receipt for £75. We made arrangements to meet with both Mrs Cook and Ian Evans to get the original receipts.

We looked back to the beginning of the new book: fifteen sales all for £25. We added the number of sheds and greenhouses sold: 21 over 15 sales. We did our sums. If he actually sold them for £75, he made £50 on each of the sheds or greenhouses—that was £1,575 in total of which he gave the allotment society £525 and pocketed the rest, £1,050. There was no receipt for the sale of the shed or greenhouse to plot A18.

Kitty wanted to call a meeting of the committee there and then but, so far, we had no evidence against him as we needed the receipts and to speak to the other people in the book.

Over the next couple of days, we met up with most of the people we had contacted on Facebook. We tried to visit all those in the book, the first being Mrs Cook who showed us the receipt given to her by John: the page number was 10 but in the real petty cash book she was number 14. She demonstrated her signature which bore no relation to the one in the book. This was repeated by Mr Evans. Some people had no receipt but insisted they had paid more than the £25 in the book and all demonstrated their signature to ensure we believed they had not signed any receipt.

The devil in me kept saying 'Tell Shane and let him deal with John Farthing' but then the nice person interjected and said 'No, Shane will end up in prison and that wouldn't help Roy or his mum!'

We decided to call a meeting of all committee members but without John Farthing. Sitting in my shed, we managed to contact all committee members bar the vicar and we arranged a meeting for the following day at my house, asking for complete confidentiality.

As we packed up to go home, we passed the vicar's plot. Pruning an apple tree, his dog collar on, with his white straw hat and green gardening apron, the picture of an English vicar in his garden at peace with the world. We stopped to ask him to attend the following day, which he agreed. We had decided that we wouldn't tell anyone the reason for the meeting in case they let it slip, but this was the vicar so we told him we felt there had been dishonesty and fraud by a member of the committee and wanted to consult with members before we took it any further. We gave him a quick précis of the problem but before we could finish he put his hand up and explained that he couldn't be involved, the church wouldn't allow it and that it would be a conflict of interest. He turned and walked to his shed. We were dumbfounded.

The whole committee met at my house the following day, minus John and the vicar. Between Kitty and me, we prepared the dining room and got some tea and biscuits on the go. We felt very pleased with ourselves. We were on the full ego trip when all six of them arrive at once. They all looked rather hostile; Bobby Bee couldn't make eye contact. There was an element of nervousness in the air and they refused tea and biscuits which is an unknown event. Somewhat taken aback by their attitude but not deterred from our mission, we made a start and managed to explain to our male colleagues our suspicions, then presented them with the actual receipts and the petty cash book, backing up our findings. They looked at each other and they began to squirm in their seats. Silence held in the air for what seemed like five minutes. Eventually, one of them broke ranks and spoke. It was Bobby Bee. He looked at each of the other committee members as if he was looking for permission; imperceptible nods were given.

'We all realised something was going on.'

Kitty and I looked at him and at each other and together we said, 'You knew?' The squirming increased.

'Yes, well, no!'

Another squirmer braved up. 'What are you talking about? You either knew or you didn't.'

'You see, it's very difficult to explain. We didn't know what to do.'

'So you just left it?'

'Well, no,' Bobby started up again. 'No, we made some enquiries and it seemed to confirm what John had suspected.'

'What *John Farthing* had suspected? John Farthing suspected something?'

'Yes,' he said, and now the squirming was being turned into a rhythmic chair dance!

'How could you? If you had, you would have found out that John was screwing the plot holders and the society.' There were beads of sweat on Bobby Bee's top lip and he looked agitated. Looking for approval once again from the others, he continued. 'That's not what we investigated.'

'What else was there to investigate?'

Bobby looked at his fellow members but they avoided eye contact. None of them spoke. 'First, before you both eat me, let me finish!'

We were too intrigued to argue—or eat him!

'Okay.'

'You see, John, John Farthing, said he had bumped into the bloke, you know, the one you got the shed and greenhouse from. Remember it was sold to The Cowboys?'

'Yes. Mr Kennedy.'

'John said that this bloke, Kennedy, told him that before John and his sons turned up to dismantle the shed and greenhouses, another member of the society turned up to see what needed to be done, a survey like . . . and they said it was a much bigger job than expected.' He fell silent; he was very rattled and the squirming increased around the table.

'And?'

134

'And that there would be a dismantling and removal charge of £50.' All the heads around the table nodded in unison.

My brain was working overtime. Charge for dismantling? This wasn't on the cards. A deafening silence hung in the air again, the squirmers waiting for a response, Kitty and I trying to understand what had been said.

'And that was John Farthing . . . the scheming,' said Kitty, 'the conniving shit. He wasn't happy conning plot holders, he was screwing the donators over. Wait until I see him! He is going to get a piece—'

Bobby interrupted her. 'No, it wasn't John!'

'Well, who was it?' I said, looking around at them all.

'Kitty!'

'Me?'

'John Farthing said Mr Kennedy gave him your description.'

'Me?'

I was transfixed. All I could say was, 'You think Kitty is on the fiddle?'

'Well, John said you were probably both in on it because you found it. That's when we decided we were out of our depths; we didn't know what to do.' The silence filled the room. I have never known silence to be so loud; gone were the two egotists, gone the smartarsed-ness. Silence—straight to simmering rage!

We sat in disbelief. They were all now speaking at once, now defending themselves, how they knew it wasn't true but wondered how they could find out either way.

'Just let me finish,' Bobby said, beginning to quiver at the thought of upsetting Kitty any further (who was now going a puce colour and starting to shake with rage). He spoke very quickly as he realised he had lit the blue touch paper, and any minute now Kitty was about to blow. 'That's when we went to see the vicar but he said to leave it alone, don't talk about it, just take my advice and leave it alone. We were at a loss, so Jock,' pointing to a fellow squirmer, 'thought we should go and see Mr Kennedy and ask him about it. I wasn't keen to do that cos if John Farthing found out, well, we know what he is like. But it was the only way we could find out for sure, so we went to see Mr Kennedy and he wasn't happy at all, felt the allotment society had duped him.' Bobby fell silent for a few seconds and now the colour had drained from his face and he was visibly sweating. He took a deep breath, but before he could continue, Jock, in his melodic Scottish lilt, jumped in. 'Aye, he was livid, I asked him to describe the person who did the survey. He said it was a woman, about fifty, with long red hair.' Kitty and I looked at each other.

'Well, it wasn't me!' Kitty said.

Jock carried on. 'She wore a long coat and flirted with him. Mr Kennedy is about eighty and on sticks, we knew it wasn't you, Kitty. You're not quite that desperate.'

'No, it wasn't me,' Kitty said, annoyed.

'We know . . .' Bobby said.

'You know?'

'Aye,' Jock continued. 'This Kennedy fella said she had *terrible* breath, the worst set of teeth he'd ever seen, well actually, just the one tooth.'

This gave Bobby time to use one of the paper serviettes to wipe the sweat from his face before carrying on. 'He also mentioned her enormous bulk and body odour.'

The squirmers began to nod and titter, Jock tried to lighten the mood. 'Aye, she'd have been more convincing if she'd put her toy teeth in.'

Kitty stood up. The squirmers began to cower, awaiting the rain of verbal abuse.

'Wanita!!! Wan-bloody-ita! He thought I was the "pickle onion stabber" Wanita?' Lots of nodding squirmers around the table, Kitty dropped back in the chair. *Dear God. Wanita?* Bobby was speaking quickly in an effort to stem the anticipated eruption!

'After that, we didn't know what to do, so we went back to the vicar and told him what we had found out and all he did was to reiterate what he said: Please just to leave it alone.'

Kitty carried on to herself as much as anyone else.

'He thought I was *Wanita*? What a fecking cheek!' smiling an exaggerated smile and showing off her magnificent molars.

'Do these *look* like pickle-stabber, tombstone teeth. *Do* they?'

I began to realise that Kitty's vanity was more important than questioning her honesty. The squirmers started to giggle.

'We just didn't know what to do so—'

'So you did nothing!' I said

'We knew it wasn't either of you but we wondered why the vicar would say that. Was he protecting John? Had John got a hold over him? We didn't know what to do for the best so yes, we did nothing. We didn't investigate the sale of the sheds as we were so hung up on the survey fees we just didn't think to look any further. We knew there had been talk about the society being on the fiddle and we thought we had found it.'

'Why didn't you tell us when you realised it was Wanita?'

'We knew it wouldn't go down too well if you found out and hoped that we could discover what was going on with John and the vicar. Then tell you.'

Kitty was still smarting over being mistaken as Wanita. The fact that she had also been accused of fraud and stealing seemed secondary to being linked with John Farthing's foul-mouthed wife, who as well as needing urgent dental care, suffered from halitosis and excessive body odour which was exasperated by her enormous bulk, so that was far more insulting. She had a point!

Monday came and went. I had forgotten the doctors!

The Plan

We tried to work out what was happening. Was the vicar taking a stand in favour of John Farthing? We didn't know, but we both felt that we should tell the police; afterall, there had been a *crime* and people were quite rightly upset about it—the crime now was bigger than we expected. How many times had the survey taken place? Maybe our figures were underestimated by a large margin. If he and Wanita had surveyed all fifteen sales at £50 a go, that was another £750!

Various theories came forward about the vicar: John Farthing was blackmailing him about some dubious activities, the vicar was having a relationship with Wanita, followed by much laughing and coarse remarks. Was the vicar on the fiddle too? All of us doubted that the vicar was anything other than an honest man, therefore it must be related to the rules of the church. We went round in circles until, in the end, we agreed that Kitty and I would have another go at the vicar and report back by the end of the week.

The squirmers' appetite had returned and they left after drinking the tea and devouring the biscuits. They seemed calmer but still embarrassed—and quite rightly so. I can't say we were very pleased with their behaviour, but hey, we have to share the site with them and who wants to make enemies in a small community like ours? Afterall, they didn't mean any harm and they quickly realised the error of their ways. They will forever be known as the squirmers!

We met the vicar coming in the gate the next day and again asked for a word and again he refused to discuss it. We told him that we had no option but to go to the police immediately. He suggested we went to his shed for a cup of tea first.

We were in the shed for about an hour and came out to bright sunlight, shell-shocked but agreeing not to go to the police. It had gone like this:

After making the tea, offering us biscuits and checking no one was coming up his path every few minutes, he shut the shed door and began.

'There are several reasons why I would ask you not to go to the police just yet. But I must be assured of your utmost confidentiality.' After lots of nodding and agreeing he went on.

'You see, I have had concerns about *certain irregularities* at church, but I tried to dismiss it and tell myself it was a drop in the economy, or just mistakes. Anyway, Mrs Collier, you know, the owner of animal sanctuary CRAPs?' We took a quick guilty look at each other. 'She told me that there had been certain happenings at the sanctuary and came to ask my advice. I realised how the squirmers must have felt. All I could think of was the things I would do if The Crims had done something else.

'You see, our collection plate has been very low over the past few months. I told myself that this was part of the financial dip in the economy, people just haven't got the money, until one Sunday John Farthing didn't turn up to church until halfway through the service. By then I had asked one of the choir boys to collect for me, just for that day. He agreed and he was in the process of doing so when John turned up. He was furious and became insistent that he took over. He even raised his voice at the boy. The parishioners were staring at him. Mrs Harvey took particular pleasure from the scene.'

'Mrs Harvey . . .?'

'Yes, Mr and Mrs Harvey have been at the church longer than me. She looks after things, cleans and coordinates my diary, does the flowers, handles the takings for the "bring and buys" and helps me set up for weddings and funerals and so on. Mr Harvey does the gardening and handyman work. They are both well in their eighties but mentally very sharp. Mr Harvey takes the computer courses for seniors down at the community centre. They were very pleased at this scene and I can't blame them.

'To placate John, I told him he could resume normal service next week. He wasn't happy but agreed. The difference in the plate was noticeable, it was nearly £100. £65 up on the Sunday before and all Sundays for the past six months. It was back to what we would have expected in the old days or, should I say, before John started to do the collections.' As an aside, he added, 'Prior to that, John was attending St Stephen's but the vicar passed away and he didn't like the new female vicar so he started to come here. We have carried on with the normal Sunday routine since then, however, I have set wheels in motion.' He took a sip of his tea and gave a deep sigh.

'What about the Harveys?' Kitty reminded him.

'Ah, the Harveys, yes. You see, a few weeks earlier we had a bring and buy sale which brings in much needed funds for the church, usually around £300. Sometimes people donate expensive items and Mr Harvey will look them up on the internet and we raffle them or ask a good price for them. As I said, Mrs Harvey usually handles all the money and cashes up at the end of the day but this year John Farthing was on hand to assist— much to Mrs Harvey's annoyance.'

Another deep sigh and he continued, 'A few days before the event, John came to see me and told me of his concerns about Mrs Harvey's memory, of her leaving the vestry door open. He gave me a bag of coins he found in the kitchen. He didn't know where they had come from but thought I should have them.'

Kitty broke in. 'Ah, the old sprat to catch mackerel trick.' I looked at her; she sounded like someone out of a 1930s detective movie.

'Yes exactly, he also said that there were rumours that Mrs Harvey was asked to leave the local supermarket as she forgot to mention the bottle of port in her bag when paying at the till. This was totally out of character for Mrs Harvey but things have been happening. I told him about the candlesticks.'

'Sorry, Vicar, candlesticks?'

'Yes, the candlesticks. A few weeks earlier, I realised the silver candlesticks were missing from the vestry cupboard and I asked Mr and Mrs Harvey about them. Mrs Harvey thought they were still in the cupboard as usual, but she couldn't find her key. They weren't there and now we don't know where they are, or her set of keys. I should have alerted the police or the bishop then. I asked John had he seen them but he said no, that he should give the church a thorough search before calling anyone in as we didn't want to get her into trouble just because of a poor memory, and I agreed.'

'Were they valuable?'

'Yes, very. Sixteenth century, solid silver. We both searched the church, the grounds and the vestry umpteen times. You see, after what John said about Mrs Harvey with the port and now the keys, it cast a shadow over her mental state. I look back now and realise how stupid and gullible I have been. I was going to inform the bishop but John suggested we wait as they would probably turn up and spare Mrs Harvey any further embarrassment. Also, to ensure the "bring and buy" went to plan, he suggested he shadow Mrs Harvey on the day and I agreed.'

The vicar fell silent, I couldn't help but feel very sorry for him. Kitty broke the silence.

'Well manoeuvred, Mr Farthing. And you don't want us to go to the police until you have told the bishop about the candlesticks?'

He carried on as though not hearing Kitty.

'After the event, Mr Harvey came to me and asked did I know what had happened to the solid gold fob watch donated by Major Simpkins. The Major had been on the phone to ask how much we raised on it. I knew nothing about it. Evidently, prior to the event, the Major had rung Mr Harvey to let him know it was valuable and to keep an eye out for it and that it had been placed in a small red box inside a larger box of jewellery items but clearly marked for his attention. He had looked for it but it wasn't there and I have asked around and no one knows what happened to the watch—it has never been seen.'

Kitty broke in again. 'How were the takings on the day?'

'Abysmal, just over £120 and most of that was on the tea and cakes. Then after the conversation with Mrs Collier, well . . .' He sat quietly for a few moments, staring at the bottom of the cup, turning it slightly as though he was about to read the leaves.

We were both enthralled. Could this man get any worse?

'Mrs Collier? Who is Mrs Collier again?' I asked.

'CRAPs,' Kitty said, nudging me.

'I am sure I am not speaking out of turn when I tell you the animal sanctuary has been struggling financially over the past few months. Their insurance has gone sky high as they have had a spate of attempted burglaries lately and have been told by their insurance company to improve their security or they will be refused cover.' My stomach plummeted. The tea leaves took his attention again and, as though talking to himself, he continued.

'John does voluntary work with the Sea Cadets and about six months ago volunteered at CRAPs too. At first, Mrs Collier thought he was a godsend, cleaning the back rooms out, feeding and cleaning the cages, getting the cadets involved with helping around the grounds. It was John who suggested and organised to raise much needed funds by packing bags at Asda

146

in return for small donations placed in a bucket. He even went to the wholesalers and bought ten buckets and had the labels printed with the names and logo on the front so there would be no misunderstanding who they were donating to.' We were silent, no point in trying to hurry him up. 'They raised approximately £50 a day and Mrs Collier thought this was good until she went to a conference on Fundraising for Charities. It was a thoroughly boring day until they gave information on best ways of raising money. Bucket collections were very high on the list, the average amount from a day's bucket collection was between £350 and £800. It made her think, but she convinced herself that they were exaggerating as they tend to do at these events. However, it did make her think. But ten buckets went out and ten came back they hadn't been opened or tampered with so she told herself that maybe people just didn't like CRAPs and didn't want to give. The next week was the turn of another charity and she happened to be shopping at the same time as they were collecting, so she made it her business to find the person in charge and ask a few choice questions. She was astounded to find out that on an average Saturday, they took between £400 and £500 each time they did this supermarket.'

Kitty jumped in. 'They must have been tampered with, there's no other way it can be done!'

'No, they hadn't, but Mrs Collier spoke to her accountant and now has a fair idea how it was done, and she too has put a plan in place to confirm it.'

Kitty and I sat looking dumb, waiting to see if there were any other revelations coming our way. After another long stare into the tea leaves, he carried on.

'Can you prove that he has been robbing the plot holders?'

'Yes, beyond doubt, plus we have people who will make statements.'

'If you go to the police now, he'll be alerted. *We* will not be able to prove beyond doubt that he has robbed both the church and CRAPs.'

'Which is why you advised us not to go to the police, until you have 100% proof?'

'Yes!'

We had to wait.

In the Meantime

The first couple of times on Skype, I wanted to explain Roy to my family but it was difficult to do when Roy was sitting next to me. But now I was able to use the computer and get Skype up and running all by myself and was quite excited. Why didn't I do this before now?

It took me a couple of tries but eventually I got through. We sat and talked for over thirty minutes, Megan coming and going out of the room, shouting to me as she walked through, sometimes sitting and chatting then running off to get something to show me. I told Emma and Alan all about John Farthing, the crimes he had committed. They were fascinated and loved it. Emma said if this was on the television you would say it was ridiculous and farfetched. I hadn't got to Roy yet.

I tried to tell her quietly about Roy, that I really wanted to do something in return for Roy's kindness, trying to be careful and not talking about his homosexuality and dressing up in ladies' clothes in case Megan heard. So each time she entered the room or passed by I changed the subject, assuming she hadn't heard, until she put her head in front of Emma's and said, 'Nana, Roy is gay and all gays love dressing up and parading round so you should help make the outfits. Gays love all that pride thing and if he misses out he will be PO'd,' then removed herself from the screen as quickly as she had appeared. I was astonished and was about to start making excuses when Emma jumped in with, 'What a good idea Megan . . . and you *are* a good sewer, mum!' No alarm in Emma that her daughter of twelve understood and could comment on gay people, or that she had just used shorthand swearing—just supporting what she had said.

I was taken aback. I was beginning to see how different this world was to when I was twelve years old; machines that can answer any question in any language in seconds, that will allow you to talk to people thousands of miles away as though you were in the room together. The only method of communication I had as a child was to write a letter or the phone box at the end of the street that you needed to put in four pennies to speak for three minutes and was only used in extreme cases, never just to talk to someone.

As for homosexuality, as a child and an adult I didn't know what it was. I had heard muted comments like 'one of those' or 'queer'. I was married and had a baby before Harry explained homosexuality to me. The world had moved at an astonishing rate since then and now my granddaughter, a twelve-year-old, not only understands about homosexuality but feels confident enough to talk openly about it in front of her parents and give her grandmother advice about it!

The following day, I rang Roy and asked him to call in after college. I phoned Kitty and told her my idea. I thought there were about three very fancy outfits to make and I needed help. The next morning, she came with her sewing machine and we set them both up on the table in the dining room which was now becoming a very versatile room.

Roy arrived just after 4 pm, looking somewhat depressed. I took him into the kitchen, made a cup of tea and asked had there been any developments about POPs. He said he had res-cued most of the material, some of the feathers were bent and unusable and the sewing machine had broken into several pieces, some of which couldn't be found. Kitty arrived as the tea was made and followed us into the kitchen with an excited air about her. I poured the tea out, put out a plate of chocolate biscuits and put them on a tray, and ordered them both to the dining room. Roy sat at the table and started to push the machines away in order that I could put the tray down. We both stood staring at him and he looked blank.

Kitty asked, 'When is POPs, then?'
'May Bank Holiday weekend.'
'How many costumes were you making?'
'Just the three.'
'Just three?'
'And dress the float, but Wayne was lending a hand with that.'
'We only have two sewing machines?' Kitty said, looking from me to Roy. Realisation eventually hit Roy and his eyes lit up and he jumped up and clapped his hands.
'The hardest thing is the sequins, they have to be handsewn but Col has a very gentle touch—great for sequins. The headdresses, they're a nightmare to make, the tails, well, they are Jerri's forte!'

Roy was in full camp mode now. We laughed and suggested that his friends might like to help.
'Can they? Shall I ring them? I will, I will ring Jerri and Col, right now.'

Within minutes he was ringing Jerri and Col to come and meet the team and for their first measure. Jerri was straightforward, if I can use that phrase, Col not so much.

'I know, Colli. Yes, I know, but that was a couple of weeks ago, love. And you know you have a tendency, don't you?' then, 'I know it's your hormones, love, but we don't want a repeat of last year's panto, do we? It was like trying to pour instant whip into a straw.' Silence for a minute while he nodded. He started with the address but was interrupted again.

'Yes, you can use Mrs L's lounge,' nodding in my direction. I nodded back.

'No, no one apart from you, me and Jerri.' Silence. 'No one,' again. 'Mrs L and Kitty.' Silence. 'But it's Mrs L's house, love.' Silence. 'It's Kitty's sewing machine and she . . . no, they are just helping us make the outfits.' Silence. 'They are just old ladies from the allotments.'

Kitty and I looked at each other.

'No, I know you didn't know.' Silence. 'Yes, of course.' Silence. 'But it was a tiny one and you were going at it ten to the dozen, it was bound to swell up, it looked very sore.' Silence. 'Yes, my favourite too,' and hung up.

He looked at us and rolled his eyes to the ceiling. 'He is so precious at times, honestly, he really does think he is the only gay in town.'

First the magic world of the new world with its new method of communication. Now we had entered into an alternative world of gays and trannys. I was nearly seventy, could I cope? Yes, no probs.

We began making notes on the outfits, making arrangements to work most evenings and the two remaining weekends. Roy went onto his emails and downloaded the designs he had sent to Col and Jerri. They were taken from Sunday Night at the London Palladium in the 1960s. The outfits were lovely, I just hoped we were up to the job.

Jerri arrived; he pecked Roy on each cheek. He was a very similar build, blond, not quite as tall. I could see him as a Tiller Girl: he had the right build, statuesque with a slight frame, pale face and long hair.

Col arrived on his motorbike. Roy jumped up at the sound of the bike. 'Here is Colli!' I could hear the clapping again as I opened the front door. Colli dismounted his motorbike and walked to the front door; he was clad in leathers, a big leather bag strapped across his chest, and had bow legs. Before he took his helmet off, I knew what was coming—a five o'clock shadow, tattoos and a gold earring.

154

He was very masculine; he looked like he had been in the first line as a scrum half for most of his youth and had a battle-weary nose, ears and face to match. He saw the other two and minced over to them, arms outstretched saying, 'Oh luvvies, this is marvellous, we're on the road again,' giving them a big hug.

Kitty and I stared at each other. Col was a very different kettle of fish, very manly but so effeminate, with a soft voice and a mincing walk. If you saw him coming towards you on a dark night, clad in all leather, you would turn and run, but you can't tell a book by its cover. He took off the bag and put it on the chair, brought out a pretty box, opened it and removed the tissue paper and displayed a large selection of porcelain thimbles, some with bees on them and some with flowers.

'Take your pick, boys, but this one is mine,' picking a sweet little thimble, popping it onto his very chubby middle finger and waving it round. 'No more swollen fingers for my dears!' They all laughed and delved into the bag, drooling over the contents, oohing and aahing whilst picking one each. Col came over to the little old ladies from the allotments and gave us a bear-like hug, thanking us and explaining about his collection of over 130 thimbles from all over the world and would we like to use one tonight. This was obviously a great privilege.

155

Of the three of them, he looked the most manly but he was the most effeminate, the campest and the gayest—he would be a dreadful Tiller. But this wasn't our show and they all knew what they were doing and who was doing it before we came along.

Col insisted that we had a plan with a list of tasks: who was doing what and by what time. Then, when a task was completed, it was crossed off the list. He was the organiser.

For the next two weeks, we sat round my dining table, cutting and sewing, pasting feathers, winding headdresses. During the day, we searched the charity shops for gloves and large high heel shoes that could be "improved", but at size 10 and 11 it was an impossible task. One of the most difficult things to deal with at first was Roy and Jerri's ability to strip at a moment's notice without batting an eyelid. Inhibition, modesty or British reserve were not words they understood or cared about. Kitty and I had a mountain to climb in terms of expectation and adjustment. Watching two men stripping down to their thongs at every opportunity wasn't what we expected; staying that way until the bitter end, we had to adjust—and that didn't come easy.

156

Roy bought dancing shoes on the other "new world", the internet. I was relieved not to have to go shopping with the three of them again as they would get so excited in ladies' shops and strip in a heartbeat. They would bombard customers with advice about clothes that would or wouldn't suit them; they had the ability to insult you as though they were doing you a favour and get away with it!

'May I?' Col said to a little old lady in War on Want charity shop who was considering a long, red, double-breasted cardigan. He took the cardigan off her and, with sweeping hands, walked her to the long mirror in the corner of the shop, then placed the red cardigan in front of her ample proportions as he proceeded with his advice.

'With your hair and pale complexion,' pointing at the image in the mirror, 'my dear, this cardi is going to make you look huge. A double-breasted jacket will hang over the *larger* areas, making you look even bigger. They are only for the slim, dear. Ladies larger in the bosom area need edge-to-edge or, better still, waterfalls. Red is such a no-no for you. You'd look like a huge zit ready to burst.'

I was waiting for the sound of flesh on flesh as she slapped him—instead she was like a lamb. He walked her back to the rails and selected another cardigan in blue. 'Now, this blue will match your lovely blues eyes . . .', smiling sweetly at her and without taking breath, '. . . and take the emphasis off your red veins,' making a circling motion round her face with his finger. 'Come on, let's try it on.' He picked up a cream scarf en route to the mirror and draped it over the cardi. She was very pleased with the effect and bought the cardigan for £3, and the manageress gave her the scarf free out of embarrassment.

The changing room was just an alcove with a bathroom rail and curtain pulled over that stopped about eighteen inches from the floor. This didn't stop the three of them picking dresses, trying to get inside the curtain all at once to try them on or give each other advice. They had no sense of other people around them in the shop or their modesty. They were only interested in trying on the most feminine clothes they could find—the more bling the better.

'Oh, you must try it on.' They were piling into the dressing room and giggling, trousers and jeans falling to the floor, followed by suspect frilly underwear—all of it dropping around men's feet and ankles—, whilst perching on red-painted tiptoes to get the best effect, bits of body being exposed as they moved.

'Oh, that's lovely on you.' Sigh. 'It's so you, Roy, isn't it Jez-za?'

'Well jell, darling, well jell.'

'Bit tight here. Just pat it down . . . no, no pull it . . . a bit more, yes, that's it . . . oh, fabulous . . . now take your hand out, Col-li!'

'I was just beginning to enjoy it!' followed by squeals of delight.

'Show Mrs L. Come on, prance, darling, prance.'

Two ladies, who had just come into the shop and started to root round the clothing rails, gave up pretending they weren't listening and just stood and stared at the contortions inside the curtain.

Roy appeared, dressed in a strapless, flowing, shimmering black, floor-length dress. One hand in the air and the other balanced on his hip, he struck a pose. It fitted him perfectly; even "Misery the manageress" began to soften and admitted she would kill for his figure. The two old ladies applauded. Only the upper halves of Jerri and Col's naked bodies appeared, wrapping the curtain around themselves and trying to clap Roy and get dressed.

'I am so going to wear this on Friday,' Roy said, then, picking up some ladies' socks and stuffing them down the front of the dress, he pranced to the mirror in the corner, modelling the dress as he went.

Jerri disappeared back inside the curtain, then a few minutes later he flung the curtain back and, with legs that any woman would have killed for, strutted out wearing a tightfitting, very short red cocktail number with a matching scarf. He walked over to Roy and studied his dress in the mirror; after looking at his backside, he decided that it was too big round the rear end. Col popped his head out of the curtain and gave it the once over, saying, 'We can fix that,' then pranced out of the curtain, his upper body and tattoos for the entire world to see. 'Could I have some pins, please?' which Misery gave him. With a few quick tucks at the side, it was very tight. Just the look Jerri was going for. Col was half dressed with the vivid purple jumpsuit pulled up to his waist.

All three of them piled back inside the curtain. Jerri appeared again and sorted through the jewellery section, then disap-peared inside again. Misery threw me a look of 'oh, this is go-ing to be bad' and I was mentally rehearsing an 'oh, that's lovely' look in place of the 'oh God, that's awful' look when

160

Col emerged. He had wrapped the pashmina loosely round his manly shoulders, just letting one side drop a little longer which gave the look of slimness. The pants were very loosely fitted and flowed nicely as he walked, hiding his bow legs. Jerri had found him a long chain necklace that fell well below the waist, again giving the look of long and slim. I was surprised how good he looked, he definitely had a flare with clothes. He managed to hide his bow legs, and if he shaved his hairy chest and covered the tattoos with makeup it would all look better again. I was pleased and relieved; Misery and I gave each other a 'well I never' look.

Roy and Jerri were clapping him and saying, 'You look gorge, Col, just gorge.' This was followed by an impromptu and much exaggerated catwalk around the shop for customers and staff. Roy picked up a folded umbrella, and as he and Jerri followed Col mincing about the shop, he began to speak into it. 'Homos, transgender, straights and gays, today we have Collette who has especially flown over from Paris for today's show. She is looking gorge in a little purple number teamed with chain necklace—chains are so in this year, ladies. Collette's pashmina is handmade from . . .' He stopped to read the label, '. . . China.' He was interrupted by the shop door opening: an old man with a very bad stoop was using a stick to open it and stepped inside the shop. They all fell silent, frozen in position. He slowly looked up and, seeing the three of them in full camp mode, without any change in expression looked down and backed out, muttering to himself, 'These bloody pills, wait until I see the doctor. First the shits, now I'm hallucinating,' closing the door behind him. The two lady customers laughed and applauded and even Misery managed a smile.

As I drove them home, we were all giggling and laughing and I complimented Col on his taste in clothes, that the outfit fitted him perfectly. He replied, 'Yes, and when I get back I'm going to slit the seams on the pants up to the hips so I can show off my legs, and with fishnet tights that'll be—'
'Oooh!' Roy was clapping in his boyish way.
Jerri jumped in with, 'Oooh, that'll be gorge, just gorge, Col.'
I found it hard to concentrate on the road.

Their Tales

All the outfits were basically the same: long satin gloves, tight-fitting bodices with silver sequins, each with extra coloured sequins mingled in. Roy had red sequins sewn in, Jerri had yellow and Col had black. We would link the extra colours with the plumes in their headdresses and tails so each would be slightly different. Col did have a gift for sewing; he had nimble fingers and sewed better and faster than any of us.

After measuring them all, we wondered how we could make one size fit all. We came up with the idea to use a sewing pattern for a swimming costume as a template for all three. Roy and Jerri were roughly a size 12 but Col was 18 plus. We selected a stretchy fabric that is more giving and kinder to the fuller figure. The biggest problem was the crotch area—how one could hide the "male bulge" and what to do if they wanted to go to the toilet. The latter meant an opening of the fabric in that area so we made an extension to the back and front sections so they would overlap. Initially, we hoped Velcro would keep them together but this caught bits of flesh and hair and any quick movement burst the fabric open so we opted for press studs. Press studs weren't brilliant either; putting pressure on that area was a delicate operation and often brought cries of pain. The "male bulge" was disguised by sewing a two-inch fringe of tassels along the edge of the legs of the bodice, allowing us to broaden the width. The effect was quite successful, although there was cries of frustration as the tassels got caught in the press studs along with bits of body. We also had to get used to inserting fingers into their crotch areas to test the studs and tassels whilst being worn. At first, this was embarrassing, but in time it became a standing joke with Roy's crack of 'that's the first time I've had a woman's hand in my crochet'. They howled with laughter and he received a swift smack on his backside before trying to bring the comments up to an acceptable level.

As we sat sewing of an evening, we listened to them and their tales: some them made us cry with laughter but the very sad tales of them coming to terms with people's prejudices, of having to tell their parents and families of their homosexuality and their response, just made us cry.

Roy told us more about how he told his mum and two brothers. It came as no surprise to them but actually saying it out loud was very difficult. He said he had practised in the mirror for weeks before, but after a drunken night out just blurted it out and no one was upset about it. But that was life before Shane came to live back home.

At that stage, Shane had bought a house with his girlfriend. They had a baby and Shane was very busy trying to build up his community transport business. He had just got a contract with the local council to pick up disabled children and adults from home and take them to a day centre, collecting them in the afternoon and returning them home. He had three small buses and employed five people and was doing well. He wasn't really taking much notice of Roy's news, just saying 'tell us something we didn't know'. Shane had always been quick tempered but seemed to be more settled now with his house, his girlfriend, a baby and his own business. He was putting a lot of time into the business and working every hour God sent. It was a relief that he was so preoccupied—it had practically passed without impact.

It all came to a sudden halt and before long Shane was back home. He had gone to start work early one day as one of the drivers was off saying he had a hospital appointment, leaving Shane one man down. So Shane had to drive one of the coaches for the day, taking disabled kids to and from schools or day centres. After a poor night's sleep worrying about the business, he overslept the next day, and after quickly dressing and shaving and without eating or drinking, he left in a hurry, leaving his girlfriend in bed asleep.

He drove the coach and, with the help of a carer, picked eight kids up from various homes and then dropped them at school. He was en route to pick another group of disabled adults up and take them to the day centre when a message came through to the carer—that the day centre had been closed for the day as the heating was off and to cancel the pickups. It was then that Shane realised he had left his phone at home. He set off back to the office with the intention of dropping the carer off before going home to get his phone and something to eat. There were roadworks on the way back so he had to take a longer route that took him down the narrow streets that he knew went past his house. As he was passing, he decided to pop in and get his phone. Whilst parking the bus, he recognised a car that was parked a few doors down from his house. He parked and let himself in and went straight upstairs, two at a time.

He found the driver, who had taken the day off for his appointment at the hospital, in bed with his girlfriend. Shane beat the living daylights out of the driver, putting him in hospital. He was arrested and charged with assault. This lost him the contract with the council. The girlfriend got a restraining order on him and he was ordered not to go within a mile of her, the baby or the house. With no contracts and being charged, loans on the coaches and a five-year lease hanging over him, he had no choice but to put the business into liquidation.

The girlfriend was named on the mortgage of the house and agreed to buy him out at a much-reduced price. He was advised to take the offer and use the money to pay outstanding tax, having no choice but to move back home. Once Shane signed for the mortgage, the driver moved into the house with the girlfriend. Wayne had managed to get him a job as a driver with his building company but Shane was a very angry man and for any reason would go off like a bottle of pop. He used the shed incident as the perfect reason to explode at Roy.

It was a few weeks after that they heard the assets of the company had been bought by the driver at a knockdown price and the council renewed the contract with the new owners, the driver and his girlfriend. We all protested and argued that this was impossible but Col, in his quiet business-like manner, assured us that not only was it possible but common practice. No wonder Shane was a bitter, angry man.

Jerri was brought up by his grandad. His parents both died in a car crash when he was ten years old. Aged seventeen, adult enough to tell his ageing grandad that he was gay, he braced himself one day at the kitchen table and told him. His grand-dad went mad and battered him, then promptly fell asleep on the couch. The next day, his grandad was as nice as pie and never mentioned it. Jerri realised that he had forgotten the at-tack, and after a few days asked him what he thought of gays. His grandad laughed and said, 'Load of perverts, should be locked up every one of them. That's what they used to do, you know.' Some weeks later, his grandad left the frying pan on the stove and went to the pub. Jerri came home to find the kitchen alight. His grandad had dementia; Jerri had looked af-ter him for five years until one day he went out shopping and when he came back his grandad was on the floor having had a massive stroke. He was rushed to hospital but never recovered. Jerri blamed himself for leaving him. We all said the same thing: 'It would have happened anyway and there wasn't much you could do except call an ambulance.' He was upset just talking about it.

Of all the cases, Col's was the saddest. He had a private educa-tion and was clever academically; his parents were in the army and travelled abroad so he was sent to a boarding school which

168

he hated. He was expected to play rugby but hated all sports, and was seriously bullied by the other students and rugby players. He was told regularly that he was a great disappointment to his army rugby-playing father. As soon as Col left boarding school, his dad forced him into the army 'to make a man of him', where he was beaten on a regular basis and intimidated because of his sexuality, until he was discharged on medical grounds.

Then, in an effort to win favour and to placate his bully of a father, he agreed to marry the daughter of his father's friend, thinking nothing could be as bad as the army. She was a very ill-natured, unattractive daughter and she didn't want to marry him any more than he did her. She looked like Bella Emburg but it didn't matter; he knew he was gay and, so long as he could keep a distance between them, he convinced himself it would be okay.

He had qualified as an accountant by that time, specialising in charitable companies, and he kept away from his wife by burying himself in his work. By the time he was thirty-four, he had his own accountancy business. His wife knew he was gay and set out to humiliate him whenever possible, embarrassing him in public, bullying him into giving her expensive gifts, spending the money he had accrued and threatening to reveal all to his father if he refused to agree to her wants—a threat that was worse than death.

She took lavish holidays with other men, bought a home abroad ensuring it was in her name, and he didn't mind so long as she stayed there and left him alone. Eventually, it all caught up with him: he was broke, in debt, very depressed and the only thing he had was his business which was about to collapse. He took an overdose of pills. When he came round in hospital, they were lovely to him; they gave him help and counselling, they understood him, and when he said he didn't want to speak to his father or his wife, they understood. He said he realised then that that was the first kindness he could remember. He was in hospital for a few weeks, but before he came out he was put in touch with a gay support group—which is how he met Roy and Jerri. They visited him and helped him find a place to live. When he finally came out of hospital, he came out as a gay man and the three have remained firm friends since. With his confidence growing, he decided to write to his father and tell him the truth. He never expected an answer and he never got one. He was now visibly upset by the memory, and both Kitty and I were near to tears.

Jerri and Roy knew Col's story and were both upset for him; when he had finished, Roy leaned over to put his head on Col's shoulder, Jerri rubbing his arm gently. The understanding and support was palpable. Was it this—the coming to terms with their homosexuality, the broken families, the prejudices, the suffering they have encountered—that had created the strong bond that exists between these three men?

Col gained his composure and continued telling us about his business which had virtually collapsed. With the help of others, he managed to redeem it, but not before he had his marriage annulled, agreeing to let her keep everything. His business is now back on course and he has been openly gay for about three years. But this POPs festival was to be his first public event, it was a massive thing for him. To stand on the float and be paraded round town was an enormous personal step.

Without a word being said between Kitty and I, we knew his costume had to be the best.

Defining Taste

With *us two* being women alongside three males who wanted to look as feminine as possible, this fact alone put us in a good position to advise them on just how to achieve it and how to enhance the good—and hide the not so good. We all have different tastes, none more so than three gay men who want to dress up as dancers and prance about on the back of a builder's truck.

In order to make Col's costume, we went to a great deal of effort, searching on the internet and researching the variations of Tiller outfits. Some had little shoulder cloaks and theatrical masks. To cover the tattoos on his arms, we wanted to sew black chiffon sleeves into the outfit which hooked onto the index fingers with massive rings. We went to the theatrical shop and managed to get eye masks on wands and made a pilot version for them. Then, full of our own self-importance and 'aren't we the clever ones', that evening we presented our ideas: firstly, the mask.

There was a big smile and a quick shake of the head by all three and, 'Why hide these good looks?' from Col.

172

'I will be too busy throwing kisses to the admiring crowd to hold it,' from Jerri. Roy just nodded and smiled sweetly. We put the mask down, never to be brought up again. Not deterred from this slap down, we showed the chiffon sleeves idea to Col. He looked at us in amazement, saying, 'But it would hide my tattoos.'

Kitty and I looked at each other. I wanted to say 'isn't that a good thing?' but remained silent, when Roy piped up, patting Cols arms, and said, 'Oooh no, can't do that! Can't hide his best features, can we, Col?' Col preened.

During the days leading up to the event, we had the first of many visits from Wayne and his mum—but no Shane. The first time I saw them approaching the front door I chased all three boys into the lounge to get dressed. I doubted Wayne, as big and strong as he was, was big and strong enough to withstand three gay men in their frillies.

Eventually, this rule was broken as both Wayne and his mum wanted to see the outfits, and before I could protest they were down to their frillies. Col did go into the lounge and change into his outfit, but when the display was over they took the outfits off and modestly pulled on T-shirts; Col pranced around in this red kimono.

173

The truck was being borrowed from the building firm Wayne worked for. He convinced his boss that the free advertising and looking extremely "PC" would have a very positive impact on his building company. He grudgingly lent him an old flat-back truck that was covered in building dust, bits of paint, cement and plaster dust, not to mention a few dints here and there. We discussed ways in which the back of the truck could be dressed up to represent the stage of the London Palladium, but the truck wouldn't be available until the Saturday before, not giving him much time to fit it out. We were all concerned that we wouldn't make the deadline, which was for everyone to be on the float ready to leave the POPs car park at 12 noon on May Day. We needed more help in getting the truck ready. The sewing was on time as the boys were good at it, especially Col; but Roy and Jerri were slow and at any opportunity they digressed as they "needed" to strip and try everything on ten times a night.

They took photos of every stage of "The Creation of the Creations" as they called it. We had to stop and let all three cuddle up while they took selfies to show on their Facebook pages when the event was over (not now, as someone else may pinch their ideas).

Col started off being shy and getting changed in my lounge. After a couple of days, he brought a beautiful red and black kimono. Roy and Jerri didn't know what "inhibition" meant; they would be sitting round in ladies' underwear or thongs, not in the least bit bothered. My mind kept slipping back to Harry and the days we sat around that table having family meals and playing games; even the piano got played in them days, now it just sits there as a piece of memory. If Harry was here now, what would he say?

There was no point in suggesting that we ask Shane to help out as we knew what his response would be. Although, if Shane knew about how wrong he was about Roy and the shed money, he may have helped with the float, if only out of guilt. On the other hand, there was a good chance that if Shane did know, he would beat the living daylights out of John before the court hearing. The temptation was great, but then where would we all be?

The next day, Wayne arrived with his mum. I went to make some tea, but on my return, Wayne passed me going into the garden for a smoke. A feeling of dread came over me as I watched Col in his red kimono mincing after Wayne. They hardly knew each other. I watched for a minute; I hoped Col wasn't going to make a fool of himself, as Wayne was defiantly not gay, and Col knew it. I kept on watching. Col was doing the talking and looking Wayne straight in the eye, man-to-man, and he had his full attention. Wayne's face was turning red in pure anger. It flashed through my mind that Col may need the eye mask to hide the bruises if he was making advances to Wayne. Col, on the other hand, looked calm, in control: there was a look on his face—confidence? Masculinity? I couldn't make it out.

Col returned to the dining room and sat down. I couldn't help but look at him, when I heard the front door bang. Wayne was striding down the path and away from the house. Col sat quietly and Roy looked around and said to his mum, 'What's up with our Wayne?'

'No idea, he was okay before.'

I looked at Col and he smiled sweetly back and simply said, 'I am sure things will be fine . . .' and carried on eating biscuits.

The Heart Attack

Kitty and I promised ourselves a couple of hours on the allotment on Sunday morning to try and catch up. This time of year was the time of planting out and of sowing more seeds. The sweet potato slips had at last arrived—I had almost forgotten about them. It was not the right time to plant them in the ground as we had to wait until it was warm. I put the slips in a jar and waited a couple of days, making sure they were active, and then planted them into a pot and stored them in the greenhouse until June.

I picked Kitty up and we set off full of excitement as we had hardly seen our plots for over a week. Although we had seen a lot of each other recently, we were fully focussed on the festival and didn't have much time alone, but now we could catch up on lotty "goings on" and John Farthing.

We arrived at the site to the smell of burning and, as we parked and walked to our plots, we could see the smouldering remnants of John's shed, burned to the ground, the greenhouse flat, just a pile of glass glinting in the sun. The fire brigade must have been; we could see the indents in the paths. No mercy for any plants that he had put in, they had just walked all over the beds. A slight tinge of sadness went through my mind. Kitty said, 'Well, there is some satisfaction to be had from it!'

Wayne and Shane were both working on their plot, nodding hello as they walked towards us. It was unlike Shane to be sociable but he was today; he was smiling and certainly on good form.

'Shame about John's shed,' I said.

'Yes,' he said, laughing. 'Shame he wasn't in it.' Wayne threw him a cautionary glance and Shane, with a mischievous grin, said, 'I believe you need help with our Roy's float?' We both nodded. 'Well, count me in.' Shane turned and walked back to his plot.

We both stared at Wayne in disbelief. 'How did you get him to agree?' Kitty asked.

'Sometimes he just needs a bit of give and take,' smiling to himself. 'See you tomorrow. Oh, could you make sure they are dressed . . . in proper clothes. I don't think Shane will be able to cope with them stripped!' Wayne went back to his plot and we could see the two of them tittering. I was sure I heard 'a bloody red thing, you wait'. They were laughing as though they were the best of friends. Maybe they were.

Pretty Penny had become unbearable over the past few weeks. She made stories up about the 'truth of the shed/greenhouse scandal'. She turned everything round to suit her own needs: Kitty and I were responsible. Kitty and I made the money on the sales. Kitty was having an affair with John Farthing. I had to suffer Kitty's ego which was mortified once more. We were in cahoots with John Farthing. She worked herself up to such a pitch that one day, whilst relating her views on the subject to Corner George, an ambulance was called and she was taken to the local hospital having had a mild heart attack. She was kept in for a few days but sent home on medication. Being needy was something she was very good at; she took to it like a duck to water. The allotment was given up immediately, Mick became her carer and fulltime dogsbody. Neither has been since—well, not on site.

I made the appointment with the doctor the next day and a further appointment was made with the specialist. Nothing moves quickly these days and my appointment was made for a month's time. Meanwhile, I was put on beta blockers and various other pills and told to keep taking them until told otherwise by the specialist.

179

Working It Out

At 4 pm on Monday, Kitty and I were standing at the window watching for Roy; as he came quickly up the street, almost at a jog, he was smiling away to himself.

'You can't help liking Roy, can you? If I'd have had a son, I would have liked him to be like Roy: straightforward and good-natured. He's so open. If it's going around in his head, it's on his face and out of his mouth.'

'Why can't they all be ugly and fat? It's such a waste!'

'Not sure what Harry would have thought about having a gay son, but he *is* a lovely human being, as are all three of them. And if all gay men are like that, the world's not such a bad place,' I said, more to myself than Kitty.

'If God had any brains, gay men would be short, fat and ugly. That would be a much fairer idea. Such a waste to woman-hood!'

'He is far too young for you, Kit, anyway!'

'Yeah . . . no, not really. I might become one of those . . . what d'ya call them . . . you know . . . a cobra!'

'A cougar . . . apart from him being gay, he is also a trans-dresser, if that's what they are called?'

'We could swap clothes. Gays have such good taste.'

'No, he has a much better figure than you!'

'Yeah . . . I've got clothes older than him.'

As I opened the door, he came in, nearly falling over himself; he was talking so quickly we couldn't make sense of it. Kitty and I just stood there until Roy stopped and started clapping and saying, 'Isn't it exciting?' I walked into the kitchen, smiling to myself, to get the tea and heard Kitty saying, 'Haven't got a bloody clue what you're on about, Roy!'

'The painting, Mrs L's painting. It's valuable.'

'What painting?'

'Mrs L, Mrs . . . L-L-L.' Following me into the kitchen, his excitement was making him stutter.

'Sit down, Roy, you've gone red-faced!'

Roy sat, took a deep breath and began speaking slowly, exaggerating every word as though both Kitty and I were simple.

'Your picture from the shed . . . remember? I took it to college'

'Yes,' I spoke, following his slow, exaggerated manner

'And they got it cleaned . . .?'

'Am I getting it back?'

'Yes, if you want it . . . but . . .' now smiling like a Cheshire cat, '. . . you may want to sell it?'

'Why, is it a Rembrandt or a Picasso?' Kitty said, trying to be humorous.

'No, but it *is* a Melville!'

'You are joking?' Kitty dropped into the seat next to him.

'And all that time . . . in Mrs L's shed.'

'I saw some of his work at an exhibition in Glasgow when I was a student.'

'I thought it looked good when I first saw it, but it was so dirty it was hard to tell.'

'I have been looking at it for years and never noticed. So much for my Arts degree!' laughed Kitty.

'You have an Arts degree?' They were carrying on as though I wasn't there.

'Could we just stick to the picture tale, please?' I said, interrupting them.

'When it was cleaned they could clearly see it was by Arthur Melville, and it's been sent for verification and value.' Roy started to bounce up and down on the chair and clapping.

'I thought is said *Meluille.*'

'No, Arthur Melville. Some of his works have sold for over £3,000,' said Kitty.

'One sold two years ago for over £70,000,' Roy said, clapping his hands again.

'But an airfare to Oz either way . . .' Kitty chipped in.

They were both beaming at me and each other. I couldn't speak; I suddenly felt very, very hot. The room began to move around me and the kitchen floor came up and hit me on the arm. Roy caught me before it could do any more damage.

I came round to chaos; I could hear Kitty shouting to get an ambulance and the doorbell ringing, then a man was lifting my legs up and putting pillows underneath, then taking my pulse and telling me I was okay, holding my hand. Everything was hazy. I didn't feel I was in the room; I kept coming and going and all that was going through my head was that I didn't know undertakers held your hand!

'She doesn't need an ambulance but a bit of air would be good, so stop crowding her, for God's sake! Kitty, make some tea, Roy, someone is ringing the bell again, open the door!' They both disappeared. This man was taking control. I tried to focus; all I could tell was that he was very smart, wearing a shirt and tie and a dark suit.

'They are trying to smother you with kindness,' the suit said. 'You're okay, Mrs L, you've just fainted. Just keep still for a minute and you'll be okay.' I started to shake. He took his suit jacket off and put it over me and shouted for Kitty to get some blankets. I tried to focus and get up but he put his hands on my shoulder.

'You're not getting up just yet . . . stay put and let's get you right first, eh?' He couldn't be the undertaker; he was talking to me so I must be alive. I wondered if I was the colour of boiled shite but didn't like to ask, didn't want to know only dead people are really that colour, oh, and sugar. Kitty arrived. I was wrapped in a duvet and told I was going to be okay and that I was a wimp for fainting, that when I was up and about she would kill me for scaring the living daylights out of her. So I definitely wasn't dead. I opened my eyes again; my vision was starting to return. I hardly recognised him.

'Hello, Col!'

'There, that's better,' and he gave my hand a squeeze.

Roy came into the kitchen and laid down, leaning on one elbow, and said I needed to hurry up and get better because he wanted to talk about the picture and his thoughts on it.

'Did you really tell me it was worth money?'

'Yes indeed and we need a plan!'

'Okay, that's enough, she's had too much excitement now. Leave it til she's better,' Col said. I wanted to protest but didn't feel I had the strength.

It was Jerri at the door and he was hovering in the background. I could hear his voice starting to quiver. 'Is she alright?' Roy jumped up and hugged him.

'It's okay, Jez, she's fine, just fainted,' Kitty began to tell him. The doorbell went again I could hear her swearing all the way to the door. I thought the bell must have been broken, it going all the time. Then I could hear men's voices: 'Whose is the Jag outside . . . something you're not telling us, Kitty, eh?' Then, another man's voice: 'Some motor, it's got to be all of fifty grand's worth.' I could hear Kitty interrupting him, and within a split second, a massive shadow was over me. Wayne dropped down onto his knees and, eyeing Col holding my hand, was totally bemused.

'Jesus, woman, what have you been doing?' I started to get up. 'Okay, first, just sit up for a minute, then a sit on the chair and then let's see how you are.' Col was definitely in control. 'Okay, Wayne?' looking him right in the eye for confirmation. Wayne nodded, and shoving together they helped sit me up, then after a couple of minutes, onto the chair. As I moved, the suit jacket fell to the floor. I was feeling a lot better but Col was still in control. He picked up the jacket and put it back on. He didn't look like Col anymore; he looked like a business man. After a few minutes he said, 'Okay, let's get you to the couch where you can faint any time without fear of hurting yourself,' and again, working as a team, Wayne and Col assisted me to the couch, Roy behind wrapping the duvet around me. Shane and Jerri were standing wide-eyed in the hall as they sat me down. I stared at Shane and all I could get out was, 'Hello, Shane, interesting here, isn't it?'

'It bloody is, Mrs L. What you doing for an encore?'

Wayne stood up and said, 'Not too much for a while', with his massive hand on my shoulder, 'but we know what we're doing, don't we?' looking directly at Shane.

For the second time in a week, Shane laughed out loud and said, 'Building a float for this lot!'

We all just stared at him. Col stood for a moment and put his hand out and shook Wayne's hand, then Shane's. As he did so, Shane said with admiration, 'Your motor?' Col just nodded.

Roy pushed Jerri and they pranced into the dining room with Shane and Wayne following behind to discuss the float designs. Col sat still next to me, holding my hand, and helped me sit up while Kitty went for yet more tea.

'Well, I'll go to the foot of our stairs!' An expression my mum used and one which I never understood. 'What happened to change his mind?' I asked. 'I have never seen such a change . . . you look very smart, Col?'

I was beginning to feel much better and would have liked to have got up and helped with the sewing but I knew Col wasn't having it.

'What are you saying, Mrs L, that I look like a robber's dog most of the time?'

'You look very smart and business-like is what I mean. We don't usually see you *poshed up.*'

'I've come straight from court.'

Kitty came in with the tea and caught the last sentence.

'Ooooh, what have you been up to, naughty boy?'

'No, I went in my official capacity as an accountant. I had to give evidence,' he said in a funny, snooty voice. I couldn't help but stare at him, trying to read his face—bet he could play poker!

He explained where he had been and why he had been asked to attend. That he was an accountant specialising in charitable companies and, as such, was the accountant for a number of local charities. A couple of them had approached him recently, concerned about a dramatic fall in income over the past year. It was the same story from all of them but none of them could fathom the reason. All of them were doing the same activities as they always had, overheads remained more or less steady, volunteers were on the up, but collections and takings were down.

One of these companies was owned by Mrs Collier, chair of CRAPs, where there had been an attempted break-in. They were having problems with renewing their insurance as the old gates needed replacing and a modern alarm fitting, and with the fall in takings, they couldn't afford it. She too had concerns about their collections—that if things didn't pick up they would have to close. Kitty and I looked at each other. I could feel my face redden.

When Col realised that this wasn't just one charity but a number, he became concerned and asked Mrs Collier if they had new staff or volunteers and could he have a list of names. The next day, she emailed him the list. Col contacted the other charities that had concerns and requested a list of names of staff and volunteers, asking if they were CRB checked—none of them were. They weren't working with vulnerable people so no checks were needed. One name was repeated on all the lists: John Farthing. Kitty and I could only sit and listen, astonished.

Mrs Collier also told Col about the other cases, including the local vicar and his ever-diminishing collections, plus the events at the allotments and how the society was trying to bring it out into the open. It was then that he contacted the vicar and, after a visit to the church, he and the vicar agreed not to speak of it until they could put something in place to ensure that Farthing got well and truly caught.

It was Col who suggested everyone stay quiet; he who advised on the way the collection buckets could be checked, and he who advised the church. Col already knew about Roy who had told him about Shane giving him a bad time over the shed money, but didn't realise it was the same man until the vicar told him our problems and how the committee was intent on going to the police.

He felt he couldn't say anything to Roy, Kitty or I. He knew what was going on, but when he realised that we had John Farthing, he said, 'Sewn up! Sorry for the pun.' He wanted us to hold off, though, until all the others could prove beyond doubt he was stealing on a much larger scale—to ensure he got the maximum sentence.

He knew that John Farthing had been arrested and was awaiting trial, and hoped it would all be over by now, that Shane
would have seen the error of his ways and agree to help. But
the case was listed for a month after the POPs event so he decided to confide in Wayne. 'Needs must,' he said reverting to
gay speak and throwing his hands up.

'So that was the conversation you were having with Wayne
outside?'

'Yes, I explained everything and I hoped that if he told Shane
in confidence that it wasn't Roy stealing the money, Shane
would feel a bit guilty over how he had been treating Roy and
try and make amends . . . help with the float. I knew you two
were on John Farthing's case and wanted to discuss it with
you, but there were other companies at stake.'

I was confused now and said, 'But no one has asked *us* to go to
court?' looking at Kitty who nodded.

'No, and no one was going to. The case was brought forward
and took place today. Going to court isn't the nicest experience, Mrs L, and I knew if I asked Kitty to give evidence she
would tell you. So when the vicar made his complaint to the
police about the church collections, he took Robert Johnson,
another member of the allotment committee, with him to make
the complaint on behalf of the allotment . . .' I was about to

protest but he carried on '. . . and then there is the small matter of having a heart problem,' smiling at me.

'Is there any chance of anyone getting their money back?' Kitty said.

'Not a lot, no.'

'Bastard . . . sorry, Col,' Kitty laughed.

Col smiled. 'I believe his shed and greenhouse have been vandalised? But he won't need it—he got five years.'

We could hear them laughing in the dining room. It was Shane's voice. 'If you two don't stop that, Roy, I'm tellin' ya, we're off. Not having you two nancies poncing about in ya frillies!' I held my breath waiting for the reply.

'Ignore him, Jez, you look gorge. Not like him. I've seen him in his string vest and Y-fronts, not a pretty sight!'

I looked at Col and waited, expecting an explosion any minute.

'Bleedin' hell, Jez, I've seen more fat on a butcher's pencil! Don't know who you're trying to pull but you'll need a bit more meat on ya!'

Then Wayne joined in taking the mickey. 'He's just jealous, Jez, you should see the arse on the thing he was chatting up the other night. When she walked away it was like two bull dogs fighting in a bag and she had the face to match. It was like animal rescue!'

191

Roy joined in again. 'You've got a bloody cheek. It couldn't be as bad as that thing you were drooling over the other night in the pub. Image of Anne Widdecombe. We thought she'd come touting for votes. So glad I am gay!'

Silence fell on the conversation but it was Shane who rescued it. 'He tried to pull Wanita the other day—that's how desperate he is!' Col looked at me curiously.

'Don't ask!'

'After ten pints they all look like Elle Macpherson to me!' the banter carried on.

As we sat drinking our tea and listening to the raucous laughter from the other room, I felt a lot better and Col continued, 'Further news came out in court. It appears that he had a lottery win about two months ago.'

Kitty and I looked at each other. 'How much?'

'£65,000.'

We sat in silence for a minute and as we were about to explode he continued.

'Bob told me about the committee syndicate and after the case closed we approached the police officer in charge. He said the money went in and out to his wife's account within hours. They tried to follow the money but it's been moved a few times and they've tracked it so far, but they're sure that it's been sent to an overseas account and are trying to find it—but not holding out much hope.'

We were shell-shocked!

The Picture

The next morning, I woke up at 8 am feeling rested and well. How life had changed. A couple of months before, it was 6 am and up and out. Now I would struggle to get up at 8 am; I was so busy I hardly had time for the plot, so many things going on. The boys, the float, the picture and potentially Australia . . . wow!!! That was just incredible; I told myself it hasn't happened yet, they may be wrong—or they may be right but it's only worth a couple of hundred. Better than nothing but not a trip to Australia. In the end, I decided just to shut up and enjoy each day. One thing I had realised was that if the boys and Kitty were out of my life, there would be a big hole.

When the boys eventually left that night, Kitty and I had a glass of sherry and a chat about the day. It had been one to remember, apart from the fainting. Col had stayed until he felt I was okay and then said his goodbyes as he had to return to the office to do the work he hadn't done that day. Me and Kitty sat with Jerri and Roy as they worked away, wondering what brought about the change in Shane. Neither of us told them as we thought it was Col's tale and left it to him to enlighten them.

Of all the wrong doings by John Farthing, it is the one that affects us personally that hurts the most. Kitty and I bemoaned our good or bad luck. Neither of us were wealthy; both of us could have made good use of the money and the thought that he would get to keep it really annoyed us. Yes, he would probably spend a few years behind bars, but when he got out he would still have the money. The syndicate win—we weren't going to see a penny of it. How handy that money would have been for all of us. Not a king's ransom but, for me, a big step closer to a longed-for trip to Australia.

The police had said they had contacted the lottery people and were told that any winnings were deposited into the account immediately and what happened after that was none of their concern. We had no chance of getting any of it; it had been moved out of his account as quickly as it went in, moved to Wanita's account and then God knows where it went!

Although the four lads chatted and laughed a lot, they did manage to get a design for the float and continued with sewing the sequins on the outfits. Shane and Wayne left to measure the back of the truck and decide how they were going to recreate the Palladium stage on the back of it. Shane came up with the idea to do a "Beat the Clock" game—as the float only moves at about half a mile an hour, they could have someone come on the truck and play a short game and give them a little prize.

I looked at Kitty and said, 'But they used darts. You can't use them on a travelling float, they'll have your eye out!'

Jez interrupted. 'We're going to use the little rubber-ended bow and arrows.'

'We only have two weeks, can it be done in that time?'

Roy said, 'If our Shane said he can do it, then he will do it. He is marvellous with his hands.' I said nothing.

We looked at our list of jobs to do and added "Beat the Clock". Most were complete; we were left with sewing the eternal sequins on, the headdresses to finish off and the dressing of the truck—and now "Beat the Clock". We were planning to have a rehearsal on the Saturday morning before to ensure we were going to be on time and see if there were any problems we needed to consider.

On the day, they would assemble at mine at 10 am to get dressed in their costumes, put their make up on, do their hair and be taken to the starting point in Col's car at 11.30 am. Kitty and I would go ahead and would be there to help them finish

196

putting their headdresses and tails on at POPs. Wayne and Shane would be at the starting point for 11.45 am with the dressed float in time for them to get on board and take their place in the parade. They were to be number eleven in the line-up. The POPs float headed all the floats. The boys really wanted to be nearer the beginning of the parade because people would be getting fed up by number eleven. They went over and over the reasons why they should be nearer the front but it was all done in a draw. Nonetheless, they were not happy about it. They had to be ready to move into the main parade at 12 noon. Both Wayne and Shane were going to take turns in driving the float to ensure they were equally embarrassed and their reputations were equally tainted.

There was much clapping of hands and jumping up and down. Roy, Jerri and Col were visibly excited, talking about how they would pose on the truck and wave. They needed someone to take a video of it from the truck and on the ground and should they have gladioli to throw? They dismissed this idea on the cost basis. What chance did they have of winning "best float" or "best theme"? They were going to keep their costumes on all day and all night to get as much wear as possible, wearing it for the parade party at POPs when the parade finished. Should they enter the London Pride? It went on and on. They were so excited.

As Roy left he said as soon as he had information on the picture he would let me know immediately. He asked me if I was sure I wanted to sell it. Kitty and I laughed—I definitely did! Even if it was only £1,000, it brought Australia so much closer. Both he and Kitty were convinced it would be a couple of thousand at least. I was so excited about the picture but decided not to mention it to Emma; until I had sold it I didn't want to put their hopes up.

I picked Kitty up on my way to the allotment the next day. It was promising to be a lovely spring day. Most of the seeds I had put in had hardened off and were now ready to plant out, so the next few days were important. I had managed to get the canes into a tepee for the runner beans and another for the french beans. I tried different forms of structures for the beans but the tepees seemed to be sturdier and could handle the harsh winds we get across the allotment.

I am not a lover of tomatoes but grow them for neighbours—and because everyone else does. I planted about twenty of each type: Gardeners Delight and Money Maker. There is only room for about six tomato plants and four cucumbers; I planted lettuce around the borders in the greenhouse and it was packed, so why I planted so many tomatoes is beyond me. I told myself they might not take or the insects would have them. Invariably, I ended up planting them using more compost, spending hours on them and then trying to find someone to give them to.

When the nice jobs were done, weeds were always there to keep you busy. I spent the rest of the day trying to rescue some empty beds from them and make ready for the next day's work. Many plot holders have diaries they keep and work to year after year. This day, this job, prepare beds for this plant, rotate your beds. I try to follow this good practice but end up just doing what I want to do on the day. The only things I was careful about planning were the sweet potatoes. Starting in a jar, then pots, and then in the bed of my second greenhouse. Who knows, maybe in November I will have sweet potatoes.

Kitty and I stopped for a break at about 1 pm. It is hard on the allotment if you're a woman to have too much fluid or food as there are no toilets. There is, of course, the supermarket next door but I always felt that if I used their facilities I should spend some money. Going to the toilet then became expensive.

As we had our cup of tea, Danny arrived. It wasn't like him not to be on his plot all day every day this time of year and his plot was looking overgrown and unkempt. He shouted hello and kept on walking to his shed, disappearing behind it and appearing a few minutes later carrying big pots of his lupins before putting them into his van. He made several trips. They still didn't show any signs of flowering but it was probably too early. He came over and sat down. I asked him how he was and in his strong Yorkshire accent he said, 'Nowt but middlin . . .' looking behind him as though someone was listening. He lowered his voice and continued '. . . been addlin' some brass this past couple of weeks.' It was the strangest thing looking and listening to Danny: it was like talking to two different people. When I first met Danny, I really struggled. There was the Rastafarian image he portrays: full of deadlocks, coloured hat, dark skin, wicked glint in his eyes when he gives you that tooth one space one smile. But when he speaks, it's this strong, traditional Yorkshire accent that belongs to a cap and welly-wearing farmer with a sheep dog in tow. It took me an age to work out what he actually says and what it means. What he meant on this occasion was he was okay and had been busy earning some money over the last couple of weeks.

His excuse for not being around much was that he was keeping a low profile as the notice on his shed said it should come down—but he wasn't going to do it. So he was keeping out the way and coming up early to tend his plants.

Kitty laughed and said, 'What plants? Your plot's a sight!'

Again, he was looking over his shoulder at the pots that he had left at the shed door.

'His lupins look good though,' I said. Kitty stared at them and then at Dan.

'Lupins?' she said.

'Ah well, they're nowt doing that well here, thought I'd try them at home.' He stood up quickly, went over to his shed and picked up the remaining pot and left.

'Lupins?' Kitty repeated, looking at me wide-eyed.

As usual, after college, Roy came round with Jez and we set about the eternal sequin sewing, Shane and Wayne getting on with the float. Col joined us after work, now back to himself on his bike and dressed all in leather. He amazed me and I still couldn't fathom him out: he was so gay, so camp, so manly, professional, strong and so kind and, given his background, not a bit hung up. I had never met anyone like him.

201

I had got into the habit of providing an evening meal for them if they came straight over from college or work. Me, Roy and Jez started the sewing until Col arrived and then we sat in the lounge eating a lamb stew on our knees and watching telly for an hour before we started sewing again. This was the time of day when all the TV channels decided we needed to exercise our brains. Between us we could answer some of the quiz questions but Col got most of them and could give you a bit of history around the subject. We were all in awe of his knowledge and when we admired him he would simply say 'I got the very best of education in the very worst way'. Not a lot we can say to that.

After tea, we began again on the sequins and chatted away. During the evening, Shane rang Roy, bringing him up to date on the float design, and although they couldn't get the truck until the Friday evening before, they would have it ready and bring it round to Mrs L's for a quick view and approval. He was sending Roy some designs he and Wayne had come up with so the boys could pick the one they thought the best. Roy hung up and, in seconds, his phone pinged—the pictures had arrived. It's so easy when you know how . . . I was really amazed by this new world I had stumbled into: Skype, internet and mobile phones, scanning (which I don't fully understand yet) and being able to send pictures in a second . . . amazing. The pictures looked great. Roy tried to explain to me that Shane had drawn them using a computer package. It went so far over my head but I just kept saying 'yes, right, I see'. I didn't have a clue and I could hear Kitty tittering behind me. He sent three different ones and they all agreed on the one with the big wheel against the back of the cabin. Roy confirmed this with Shane. More clapping and jumping up and down with excitement—I had to stop Kitty joining in.

Roy was still waiting to hear back from Glasgow about the painting and would let me know as soon as he knew anything. I was getting edgy about it—what if they were wrong? I would be so disappointed.

We met each evening for the following week and were nearly finished by Friday, apart from the float. We got everything ready Friday night for the dry run the following day. We could have the truck for the weekend which meant although it couldn't be dressed, it could be measured, and were assured there wouldn't be any hiccups on the day. We also wanted to drive the five-mile route to POPs then the festival route of another couple of miles.

The boys arrived at 10 am as planned. The costumes were as ready as they could be at this stage and they set about doing their hair and makeup. They put their outfits on, all except the feathers and tails. They covered them with long coats as it was a guarded secret, and although they needed do a full dry run, outfits and all, they didn't want to let anyone see yet. Once we were happy with the boys, Kitty and I went ahead as planned and waited for them and the truck at the starting point, which was the car park at the back of POPs. At last, I was going to get a look at it up close.

We waited for a few minutes before the boys turned up, closely followed by Wayne and Shane. After a few jokes and friendly banter, we got back into our vehicles and set off on the route. It all went without a hitch. We came back to mine and had a well-earned cup of tea and analysed the morning. Shane and Wayne went back to the builders' yard to make adjustments to the float before they had to take it to pieces and store it until next Saturday.

From now on, there wasn't much to do for me and Kitty as we were ahead of schedule. We just needed to pray for good weather on the day and that all went according to schedule. The weather was lovely the whole weekend and the weather people promised that we were in for two weeks of sun and warm weather.

The boys, of course, were very busy: there were facials, nails, waxing in delicate areas (because as Jez said, 'you know what pain is if your pubes get caught'), there were sun tans, hair, massages and exfoliating, not to mention the trial make up.

The organisers from POPs had been invited to speak on local radio on Monday evening and we were gathering at mine to listen to it at 7.30 pm. The boys were so excited and, I must admit, me and Kitty were too.

It was a quiet weekend so Kitty and I got on with our allotments. Things were beginning to grow. When you first put little seedlings in the ground, the seed companies suggest that you leave so much space between each plant. I generally ignore them, but just a few weeks later I was already wishing I had taken their advice; they were growing like mad and looked crowded, my beans were starting to hold hands as they didn't have enough room. I would have to thin them out and replant them somewhere else. I am good at making work for myself and even better at not taking advice. The Cowboys were nowhere to be seen, and we knew they would be working on the float so we took it upon ourselves to water their greenhouse. Plants growing in greenhouses need to be watered every day this time of year, or jam bread dead in a day.

Monday evening came and we all sat round the radio. It was like a scene from the 1950s before we had television and before computers or mobile phones were even thought of. A good evening's entertainment back then was when mum, dad, me and my brothers all sat round the radio listening to *Dan Dare* or *Quatermass* in absolute silence. My brothers on the floor, arms wrapped round their knees which were stuck under their chins, were absorbed in the radio. I was always terrified and climbed on my dad's knee; he would put his arms around me and tell me it was just a story. Nonetheless, *Quatermass* scared me to death. How anyone could be scared was ridiculous but the imagination did the rest.

We sat listening to these two men explaining how the day would go and the element of competition between floats. The winner would get an automatic place in London Pride week. There were twenty-five floats in all, each with a theme. One float would have a Jamaican steel drum band, and collections would be made along the way, raising money for local charities. Roy and Jerri got really excited at the steel band and Roy said, 'That'll be very nice after', smiling knowingly at Jerri. Col threw them a cautionary glance and the conversation stopped dead.

When they left at about 10 pm, I went to bed but couldn't sleep. I had started going to bed and sleeping right through until 8 am, unlike a few months before when I laid in bed waiting for the night to end, waiting for morning to come so I could get up.

It was the thought of a "family" that stopped me sleeping. What would happen after the parade? I rolled the thought round and round in my mind for most of the night; they were not like my Emma and Megan family but they had plugged a massive hole that I avoided thinking about. Coming home to an empty house, waiting for morning to come, I had more than the allotment to keep me busy now. Something helpful and fun and I had become so fond of them, even Kitty and I were much closer than before. And the boys, well, if they stopped coming round . . . what then? I was awake most of the night thinking it over, and things are so much worse in the dark when you're on your own, but I must have dropped off in the early morning as I was woken by the sound of the phone ringing. I begrudgingly lifted the receiver up and it was Roy.

'Why haven't you answered your mobile? Are you okay?'

I looked at the clock. It was 10.30 am. I had slept in! 'Yes, just slept in . . . everything ok?'

'I have the results of the valuation. Can I come round?'

'Now?'

'Now!'

'Okay, if you can stand the sight of me in my PJs!'

'Couldn't be much worse than your lotty outfits. See you in ten minutes.' Before I could call him a cheeky bugger he was gone.

I got up and washed my hands and face. I looked, and felt, awful. I pulled my house coat on and put the kettle on and while it boiled I tried to arrange my hair into some sort of order. I checked my mobile—there had been three calls from Roy.

Roy bounced through the door, full of life, minced into the kitchen, and sat down and smiled a massive smile at me, showing his lovely, perfect, very white teeth.

'What do you want first—the good news or the question?'

'I'll go with the question first.'

'They want to know if you want to put the picture in a London auction house or Glasgow.'

'Aren't they all just the same?'

'Well, the one coming up is a specialist sale in Glasgow and it's called *The Glasgow Boys* of which Melville was one. The London one is a really well-known house which obviously just pulls in all art dealers from all over the world.'

'So, it *is* real then?'

'Defo,' followed by minor hand-clapping. 'Now ask me the good news!'

'So, what's the good news?'

'Are you seated?' He was excited, wanting to tell me but wanting to tease me as long as possible at the same time. 'It's estimated value is . . .' (long pauses) '. . . £15,000!' I could hear the silence in the kitchen and was aware I was staring open-mouthed and there was nothing I could do about it. A full minute must have passed before Roy put his hand on my arm.

'Are you okay, Mrs L? Are you going to faint again?'

'Are you sure?' He delved into his pocket and brought out a printout of the email he had received that morning. I read it; my hand was shaking as it confirmed everything he had said.

'The decision is yours, Mrs L. Glasgow or London?'

'£15,000, *really*? I have no idea.'

'Well, I would go with London. With the internet, it doesn't really matter—if someone wants it from Hong Kong or the moon, Glasgow or London is not going to make a difference!'

'I haven't been to London for years. It would be good to go again. I can go, can't I?'

'Yes, of course. They suggested a specialist sale that's taking place next month.'

'We'll do that, then. Will you come with me?' I grabbed his hand and squeezed it so tight he squealed.

I phoned Kitty and told her. She was round in a flash but I decided not to say anything to Emma until after the sale. Just in case I woke up and found I was in a dream, or it didn't sell.

The Parade

The boys were already well ahead of time and used this time,
posing and posturing for the video camera. Kitty had been designated camera woman, and as she panned on each Tiller they
explained how they made their outfits, what went into it and
how it felt to be part of the parade. Shane phoned to say the
float was nearly ready and they would leave in fifteen minutes'
time, giving them ten minutes to get to the car park at the appointed time. After calming the boys down and telling them
how beautiful they looked, Kitty and I piled the headdresses
and tails into my car and set off for the POPs car park; Col and
the boys, doing the last-minute touch-ups, would follow behind in Col's car. All good plans, as they say.

As we got closer to the High Street, the traffic started to slow
down. We couldn't get near POPs: the roads had been cor-
doned off, we were crawling into standing traffic and we were
a good half a mile away. There were police officers turning
traffic away from the High Street.

We were moving at a snail's pace and at this rate we would
never make it on time, and neither would the float. I could feel

myself getting anxious. I was looking for a place to turn around and saw a policeman directing traffic away from the area. I wound the window down to ask if we could do a U-turn. As the policeman bent into the window, I smiled a weak, limp smile. The officer started to tell me to carry on and that we would be diverted around the High Street—then he stared at me.

'Oh, hello,' he said.

'Hello, nice to see you again.' I was getting very hot under the collar now.

'That rhubarb was lovely. My wife made crumble, the kids loved it. You know what kids are like, we couldn't get them to eat fruit at all, hell of a job, but now it's all 'can we have rhubarb crumble, Mum?''

'Call by anytime, we have loads this time of year.'

I could hear Kitty talking into the phone. 'Hang on, there's a bobby with his head in the window . . .' Then silence as someone on the other end spoke. '. . . I am trying . . . give us a minute.'

'A bus has broken down on the High Street and this parade thing is about to start. It's a real mess.'

I was trying to process the fact that Freckles had a wife and kids when I tried to explain what we were doing. Kitty was holding the phone so the boys could hear the conversation. He looked from Kitty to me. I nodded to the headdresses and tails on the back seat. I told Freckles about the boys being in the parade—that we were supposed to be meeting them with the headdresses and the float in the POPs car park and we didn't know what to do now.

'You won't get near it, it's gridlocked, absolute mayhem,' then after a moment's thought, he suggested, 'The best thing you can do is make a U-turn. Tell your friends to meet up with you at that builders' yard, McKenna's on Albion Road next to the Fire Station?'

I looked at Kitty and she repeated what was being said into the phone. 'Okay, yes they do . . .' We could hear hysterical laughter from the phone.

'Meet at their car park. Once the parade starts—when we clear the traffic —it will have been diverted to Duncan Street and then Albion Road, then back to the High Street. You'll be able to pick it up at Albion Road.'

Kitty talked into the phone. 'Did you hear that? Okay, you tell Shane and Wayne . . . okay, okay, don't get upset, I will do it.' I looked at the standing vehicles around me.

'Wait there!' Freckles, full of authority, walked to the car in front and I heard him say, 'Would you mind moving up as far as you can, sir? That's fine, thank you.' He walked past me to

213

the car behind and asked him to back up. He walked back to me and said, 'When I tell you, do a U-turn, but not until I tell you.'

Freckles waited for a gap in the traffic coming the other way and strode out into the road, putting his hand up to stop further oncoming cars. Then he pointed at us in a very commanding manner and did a larger circular motion for us to make a U-turn. I turned and we were on our way back. I wanted to kiss Freckles.

Kitty repeated it all to the boys and asked them if they knew the place. There was silence then screams of laughter—yes, they did, it was Wayne and Shane's builders' yard!

Kitty looked at me, grimacing, then phoned Shane and Wayne who were awaiting further instruction. I could hear the mixture of laughter and terrible language.

We all arrived at the builders' yard together. Col phoned the organisers and explained where we were and asked for advice and was told to wait until they rang back as they were trying to reorganise the whole parade.

We all gathered in the builders' yard, waiting. It was a beautiful sunny day, the boys dressed and preening themselves, standing on the back of the truck, Shane and Wayne getting nervous, hoping they wouldn't be seen by anyone who knew them.

After a further fifteen minutes, Col wanted to go to the loo. 'There, over there,' Shane pointed, and Col trotted across over the cobbles in his stilettos to the toilet block, trying to pop his studs as he closed the door of the *Men's* . . .

'Look at those dozy buggers, they must know it's the parade today!' Wayne pointed to their next-door neighbours. The fire officers were out with the hosepipes, washing the engines down, and the sight of the "girls" in full costume brought more than a passing wolf whistle. I could see the main man who had been the lead officer at the allotment when we had the Sugar incident.

I leaned over to Kitty and said, 'Keep your head down' and nodded in his direction.

'Oh shit. Dear God, don't let him come over . . . oooh, he is!' Both Kitty and I hid behind the back of the truck. Wayne and Shane just sidled quietly to the side of the cab out of sight, not wanting to be seen with the "girls" but wanting to hear.

He was full of macho testosterone and self-assurance, shouting and whistling, showing off in front of his mates. He adjusted his braces and, with another fire officer, walked over and leaned on the truck, weatherproof trousers held up with the braces, regulation navy T-shirts, and began to chat up Roy and Jerri. The other fire officers were still shouting and egging them on, 'go on, get in there' and such like. Wayne and Shane were listening from their hiding place and desperately trying not to laugh. Shane thought it was hilarious; he was really enjoying their stupidity.

The fire officers were so pleased with themselves, their egos on a high, especially the lead officer who was, as Wayne said later, 'giving it loads'. They were leaning on the back of the truck looking up at Jez and Roy who sat on the truck, dangling their long fishnet-clad legs over the edge, chatting them up, knowing full well the officers didn't have a clue who or what they were. That is until Col emerged out of the men's toilets with his hands clutching his crotch, shouting in his most camp voice ever, 'Roy, Roy, sweetie, could you give me a hand, my orchestras keep popping out!'

They backed away mid-sentence, just walking slowly backwards as though someone had reversed the video, staring at Col then the girls as they went. Roy and Jerri were shouting, 'We'll be back later, maybe we can meet up,' then, 'Wish us luck!' and blew kisses. The fire officers turned and walked briskly back to their colleagues, heads down and huddled into a group.

Some of the other fire officers stopped shouting and others, who were obviously not in the know, continued with, 'You're not man enough' and 'Pair of wimps!' Roy and Jerri continued to wave and blew kisses, camping it up as much as possible. The fire officers huddled closer as though for safety, silence fell and after a few quick fleeting looks in our direction the two red-faced, embarrassed officers retreated into the station amidst a hail of raucous laughter and unflattering comments.

Shane and Wayne were laughing so much and taking the mickey. Shane said, 'I haven't laughed so much in years,' then tried to control himself. 'Can you imagine their faces when they . . .' and fell into uncontrollable laughter. 'What dozy bastards, everyone knows this is POPs day,' then falling into hysterical laughter again. 'Could you imagine the fright when they . . .' once again falling into tears of laughter.

Thirty-five minutes passed and we were getting extremely fed up, when Roy's phone rang. He was told to listen out for the band as it was making its way there from another car park. They had the new route so were to fall in behind the band, and

217

then other floats would meet them along the way and fall in behind our float.

We prepared ourselves when suddenly Col said, 'We must be the first float after the band!' Then much leaping about and clapping hands. Shane and Wayne got in the cab of the truck and inched to the end of the yard, waiting to see the band float. We could hear it, the lovely tinkling sound of the drums getting closer, and people were gathering along the pavement. The boys struck up their poses on the back of the truck which had been laden with bricks, cement and burly builders the day before, but today it was the London Palladium and "Beat the Clock".

As the band float came near, we could see it was bedecked as a Caribbean-style beach scene with a bar, palm trees and dark-skinned ladies wearing floral bikinis and large floral head-dresses, waving to everyone. As they slowly passed by, Jerri and Col were shouting to them, telling them how lovely they looked. 'Bribaby, you all look fabulous and the outfits are gorge!'
'Oh, yours are amazing and the headdresses . . . oooh . . . you'll win!' Bribaby shouted back. 'See you after the parade, love you!' Jerri shouted and they all blew kisses to each other.

218

The fire officers were still hosing the engines but lost concentration and were spraying water everywhere but the engines.

Kitty nudged me and nodded to the band. There, on the biggest drum, beating the living daylights out of it, was tooth one space one, Danny, loving every minute of his fame.
'Ah . . .' Kitty said, '. . . this is what the lupins were for!' It was a while after that Kitty explained the lupins to me.

Our float fell in behind the band. The two dark-skinned beauties ran to the back of their truck and started to wave and blew kisses to Shane and Wayne. Shane swung between fascination, embarrassment and lust. Wayne was staring out of the side window, his face the colour of beetroot. Shane's uncontrollable laughter had gone and, after ten minutes of staring at the two Caribbean ladies, he had settled into the land of fascination. 'This is playing with me fuckin' head—it's seriously weird shit!' he said.

At last the parade was over and, although the day had got off to a rocky start, with the help of Freckles, it had turned out very well. Not only did the boys get their wish to be first float, they won best float and best outfits. Kitty and I managed to get some video of the day, especially at the end when the local TV station turned up and filmed the floats coming down the street. The end of the parade was when they returned down the High Street three hours later and into the back of POPs. Wayne and Shane took time to congratulate the boys and gave them half-hearted manly hugs and shook hands on their successful day.

I could feel Wayne's tension and desperation to get away; he was aware of being under constant surveillance by the number of men looking far too feminine, attractive and downright sexy. You could see confusion setting in and, before he lost all reason, he was anxious to leave. Shane was ahead of Wayne, all sense of reason gone too. He was still in the land of fascination and the scantily-dressed, dark-skinned ladies welcomed him. Kitty and I watched the scene unfold.

As soon as they were helped down from their float, they were over to them in a flash. Each was about five foot five with beautiful dark skin, their colourful bikinis showing their fabulous figures, sultry good looks with large almond-shaped eyes, and perfect white teeth. The colourful headdresses matched their bikinis and enhanced their beauty. As Almond Eyes stroked Shane's chest, looking up into his face, it was gone . . . all reason, common sense . . . gone in an instant, plummeting from his brains to a lower region and buried in a heavy layer of lust.

The second sexy Caribbean lady moved closer to Wayne who now looked like he was about to explode. She removed the headdress and shook the long, black mane of hair, then ran her fingers through it, shaking it from side to side to loosen it and letting it drape over one shoulder. She just stood staring up at Wayne who seemed to be finding it hard to swallow.

'Why don't you stay for a little drink and let me thank you for helping the boys?' Almond Eyes suggested to Shane.

'Yes, that would be lovely' Mane of Hair agreed, stepping closer to Wayne.

'F-f-fire . . . fire . . . remember the fire . . .' Wayne stuttered.

It took two steps for Wayne to be safely in the cab of the truck with the door shut before he shouted for Shane to get in and us to get in the back. The word 'f-f-fire' was Wayne's desperate attempt to remind Shane of the fire officers; even had he been able to swallow sufficiently to get the words out it wouldn't have penetrated. Shane was working on sight alone . . . hearing, brains, sense . . . gone. Only his eyes were working in conjunction with desire and they were both concentrating on Almond Eyes.

'Shane, you daft bastard, get in the truck.' Shane was immovable. Meanwhile, Col, who was observing from across the car park, shouted to Bribaby to come join him and the others. Wayne put his head out of the cab and shouted again to Shane to get in. Reluctantly, Shane did as he was told, leaving the dark beauties who blew him a kiss, turned and walked away. Neither Shane nor Wayne could resist a minute just to admire the rear view of the dusky Caribbean ladies sauntering across the car park.

'D'ya think they've got dicks?'
'How the hell would I know?'
'We could stay and find out!'
'Drive the fucking truck, Shane.' Shane put his foot down and we shot out of the car park.

Kitty and I sat in the back, stifling our laughter. I looked at the scene behind us through the side mirror. I could see Roy, Jerri and Col loving every minute of the adoration they were receiving, being hugged by everyone including Danny.

We returned to the builders' yard and helped Shane and Wayne dismantle the truck. They had found a place at the back of the yard to store the Palladium stage. The fire officers were

222

all finished and safely locked up for the day. Shane and Wayne unscrewed the stage whilst Kitty and I carried the smaller items back and forth from the truck to the back of the yard as instructed. Wayne's face was slowly returning to its normal colour. But Shane was still happy in the land of fascination.

'*Do* you though?'

'Do I what?'

'Do you think they've got dicks?'

'Yes!'

'Nah, I couldn't see . . . yer know . . . any sign of a budgie.'

'Why didn't you ask to see it?'

'Oh yeah, like, 'show us your dick, gorgeous!'. She didn't look like she had one!'

'Shane man, they're trannies, ladyboys, drag queens, dressed up puffs!'

'But she . . . was so . . .' (making curving motions).

'And *she* probably has a dick as big as yours!'

'But—'

'And *she* wouldn't be afraid to use it.' Shane opened his mouth to speak but no words came out, just a bemused look rested on his face. Shane had wiped the earlier incident of the fire officers that he found so hysterical out of his mind. It took some time for common sense and reality to return and bring him back from the land of fascination. When it did, it was followed by embarrassment. I am sure he will see the irony of the situation and would like to forget about it, but I am sure the boys will remind him at every opportunity.

The Auction

After the parade was over and everything packed away, they spent some time apologising for the swearing and shouting. We assured them we hadn't laughed so much for a while. I was not sure this is what they wanted to hear but it was the truth.

They went straight to the pub. We were invited but decided against it—couldn't stand any more excitement that day. Kitty and I went home to do a quiet tidy-up and have an early night. I still hadn't mentioned the picture to Emma and decided to keep it that way until I knew for certain what was happening.

Roy came round on Tuesday. He filled me in on all the happenings since the parade: he was delighted as the television station showed forty seconds of their float with the three of them in full view. Col had been asked to go on radio to be interviewed about the parade. Winning first prize also meant they qualified to enter the London Pride weekend and this obviously meant new outfits. Roy was over the moon and it was a job to keep him from clapping his hands until they bled, so we agreed to a debrief and to discuss "the London gig" as he was now calling it. We agreed Thursday was the favoured evening.

225

Everyone came to the debrief and it turned into more of a party than anything: the three boys brought nibbles and wine, Shane and Wayne's mum and her friend came, and Kitty and I. Col arrived on his bike in his leathers, and as I opened the door he minced in, arms stretched out, and said, 'Gorge, just gorge, we are back on the road again!' before throwing his arms around me and the boys, Shane and Wayne backing off laughing, saying, 'Enough, Col, enough!'

We laughed and joked until midnight. I explained about Freckles, the fire officers and Sugar. Kitty said, 'I hope your house never catches fire or you're done for!'
Evidently, Danny was always at POPs; although not a crossdresser himself, he loved to be with and around the "girls".

Some ideas were thrown about for London Pride. Shane and Wayne said they would ask if they could borrow the truck again for the weekend and take it down to London.

We discussed the auction: Roy, Jerri, Kitty and I decided to go together on the train. Col wanted to come but couldn't get out of yet another court case. There was much mickey-taking by

Shane and Wayne and much good-natured banter between them all—a stark change from a few weeks ago.

It was agreed that we would get the early train to London and return the same evening. As we were discussing this—such is the magic of today's communication media—Roy checked the price of the early morning trains to London and back, and it came in at nearly £200 each. That ruled Jerri and Roy out as, to students, that kind of money was beyond them, and if the painting didn't sell it would leave me close to the bone also. This brought a sombre moment to the evening but there was nothing to be done, as between the four of us it totalled nearly £800, that is without food and drink. Trying to make a joke of it, I said, 'It doesn't matter, the picture will sell or not sell with or without us. We will just have to wait for the phone call.' I said as much to cheer myself up more than anything else, as it did sound a nice day out.

Out of the corner of my eye, I could see Col and Shane with their heads together. Shane was nodding enthusiastically then seemed to be rebuked by Col and curbed his enthusiasm; they both laughed. Col put his hand up for a bit of silence and said, 'Your good friend and mine . . .', nodding to Shane who smiled back, '. . . has agreed to drive you all down in my car.

But make no mistake, if he exceeds the speed limit or damages it, he won't have any difficulty with his press studs in his crotch because there won't be anything in there!'

The auction was three long weeks away so I busied myself at the allotment, dreaming of going to Australia for Christmas. Kitty and I started having a bet on how much I would get. I just hoped I would get enough for the plane fair.

The committee meeting was the following Sunday. On the agenda was the appointment of new site secretary and the open day in July. Kitty and I did our walk about as we normally did before the meeting to glean what little information and advice there was from our fellow plot holders. It usually left us feeling negative but today Kitty and I thought that, as we had dealt with the problems, that there would be some acknowledgement, maybe a pat on the back for the committee acting on information given; but no—some things never change. Moans were all we got: 'Could have told you that years ago.' We stopped at Macca's plot to talk to him, and all he could say was, 'We all knew what was going on but no one listened,' then, 'There was more to it than has come out,' but wouldn't be drawn any further. Frustrated, Kitty and I moved on, wondering what he was talking about: what *more*, what *more*? There's no more!

We went to see Corner George and his carrots; he was talking to Pete Two Plums, explaining how he grows his carrots to win. He was delighted to see us and gave us both a bunch of sweet peas he had been picking. He then thanked us heartily for removing the competition.

'I am bound to win now . . . now that misery arse has been put away. Shame in a way—he was the only competition.' Pete was laughing.

'Well, you need all the help you can get. You just can't please some folk.' We both agreed and told him about Macca's comment.

'That'll be the metal, Farthing had that away!' Of course it just didn't penetrate with everything else. We rushed back to the metal bays and, yes, it was gone. It had been gone for some time, and somewhere in the back of my mind I knew it but was so busy on the other hidden crimes I couldn't see the obvious.

The meeting was being chaired by the vicar and started on time. At the end, we all sat around chatting in a very pleasant atmosphere without John. We decided that we would have the allotment open day in July and ask the three boys to open it, dressed in the winning outfits. I was sure they would be delighted. Bobby Bee was appointed site secretary and, as was said, he couldn't do much worse.

Finally, it was auction day. It had been the longest three weeks of my life. Shane picked Kitty and I up at 6.30 am—far too early. Roy and Jerri were in the car and wide awake. Roy had downloaded a catalogue online and gave me the copy. My painting was catalogue number 385 which meant that it would be likely go under the hammer at 2 pm. The guide price in the catalogue was £5,000 - £8,000 but that was ambitious, I thought. Roy thought it was a "come and get me price". I just hoped it sold and all this wasn't in vain. We did the guessing game; we all had to join in, Roy insisted. I found it difficult to guess as it meant getting my hopes up, possibly to be dashed, but wasn't getting let off so I plumbed for £4,000. That would cover the fare and give me money to spend on my lovely family and get my car serviced when I got back. The highest guess was from Roy at £20,000 which I laughed at.

We parked on the outskirts of London and got the train to Oxford Street with the intention of walking up to Bayswater Road to the auction house, as instructed by Col. 'Don't take my car into London. Drivers in London have one rule to drive by: Only ever look forward—ignore the mirrors, ignore all the cars at the back, and them at the side, they can look after themselves, just drive forward!' It was true, the roads were mayhem. Oxford Street was a madhouse, even the pavements were so over-crowded we couldn't walk together, we kept losing each other or getting pushed off the payment. I was glad when we reached the auction house and got safely inside. We were an hour early so Kitty and I walked around the auction house looking at the art work and antiques for sale, but we couldn't see mine.

The three boys went for a walk round to see if they could work out the information or the route the London Pride parade would take, promising to be back in plenty of time for the painting.

Kitty and I followed the signs down the stairs to the auction room where it was all happening. We managed to squeeze into two seats near the front. There were televisions on three walls, one just in front of the auctioneer the others on side walls. There was a smaller television with a list of numbers on which Kitty pointed to and whispered, 'Internet bids.' The auctioneer started on this new lot. He was talking fast: 'Lot 359 striking modern art aptly called *Life* by A.A. Williams. Her work is in much demand with a growing following, exhibitions in Paris and Rome and Sydney, a much sort after artist, the Andy Warhol of tomorrow. I can start the bidding at 10, can I say 10, £10,000?'

'Where is the picture, Kit?'

'That's it!'

'Where?'

'On the screen.'

'I can't see it.'

'£10,000, £10,500, £11,000, £12,000, £13,000 . . .'

'There, on the screen.'

'But that's a mop and bucket!'

'. . . £15,000, £16,000 . . .'

'That's it, its modern art.'

'It's shite,' Shane's voice came from behind.

Hands holding paddles were still going up—it was up to £25,000. 'Any advances, in the room going at £28,000, all done?' Then the auctioneer brought the hammer down with a flourish. A lady nearby held a paddle high in the air. No one shouted or said anything, it was all very calm. I wanted to say, 'are you sure you want to pay all that money for that?'.

Shane leaned over and said, 'I could give her a real mop and bucket for half the price.' £28,000 gone in a minute and no one batted an eye lid. We all looked at her. £28,000 for a badly-painted mop and bucket. 'She must have more money than sense,' I whispered to Kitty who was just staring at the lady with no sense (but had very nice clothes). The senseless lady and her companion stood to leave just as the boys made a last-minute entrance and pushed their way to their seats.

The next twenty-five lots went in thirty minutes. I made a quick calculation and in that thirty minutes the amount of money spent on paintings was over £750,000—a staggering amount of money. It gave me hope that mine would sell.

At last it was my painting. The porter held it above his head and there it was on the televisions. The auctioneer began with, 'An Arthur Melville painting, one of the Glasgow Boys, a rare and until recently lost painting, a beautiful beach and sea scene . . . where shall we start? I have bids on the books and on the internet so let's start at £8,000.' Paddles went up in the room: £9,500, £10,000, £11,000, telephone bid at £13,500, £14,000, £15,000. I felt hands holding mine, Shane's hand on my shoulder. Kitty was squeezing my arm. '£18,000, any further advances on £18,000, £19,000, £20,000, and more? *Sold* . . . to . . .' a paddle was being held high '. . . number 3099. The next lot is . . .' he carried on. I was numb. All I could hear were Roy

and Jerri clapping and jumping up and down and the auctioneer saying, 'Quiet, gentlemen, please!'

We squeezed our way out of the auction room. I needed air, I
felt ill, it was too much. I managed to get out into the street
with the others behind me trying to get past the people attempting to get in. I sat on the steps of the auction house and quietly
fainted.

I came round to a group of people being organised by a first
aider and I was on a bed in a room. Roy and Shane told me
that I was in a specially-adapted room at the back of the auction house. They often had such emergencies, either because
people are delighted or very disappointed, which, as the first
aider told me, happen on a regular occurrence. And they have a
doctor on standby and he was on his way; once he had cleared
me I could leave. I closed my eyes and drifted off again. Did I
really get £20,000?

By the time the doctor arrived, I was feeling a lot better and
was sitting up drinking tea. He took my blood pressure,
checked my eyes, asked questions about medication and
agreed with the first aider that it was just a faint brought on by
too much excitement.

The doctor told me to sit for another ten minutes and then, if still okay, I could go. We sat talking about our sale and wondered how much the auction house would take and when I would get my cheque. I couldn't wait to get home and Skype Emma and Megan and book the ticket and buy new clothes. I could feel myself starting to go again and had to lie back, close my eyes and relax for a minute or two to let it pass. There was a knock at the door and a young, very smartly dressed lady came in with an envelope.

'Hello, I am Tasha from the accounts department. I believe you have been unwell?'

'She just fainted again!' Kitty said.

'Well, this will make you feel better. I have brought your cheque and receipt. Are you okay to sign?'

'Oh yes, I am, how much is it?'

'After the auction house fee of 20% that leaves you with £16,000. If you would just like to sign here and here.' I could hardly write, my hands were shaking so much. All I wanted to do was to leave before they realised they had made a mistake or that it was a fake or not mine.

As we walked through the reception of the auction house we spotted the two ladies who purchased the *Life* picture. They were sipping from glasses of wine and looking at another similar piece of work. Shane being Shane walked over and started talking to them. I heard him say, 'Oh, I wanted to purchase the *Life* but today we were selling some works. You can't always buy in this business, can you? Maybe next time. We sell to re-invest on behalf of our clients . . .' We were wide-eyed at his cheek. Jerri and Roy giggled and Kitty leaned over and said, 'D'ya think he'll check them for dicks?'

The journey home was long, the weather turned nasty and the roads were very busy. We rang Col and Wayne from the car and told them the good news. They were both over the moon and made arrangements so we would meet and have a proper celebration. The weather was bad outside but it didn't stop us singing and laughing all the way home. As soon as I got home, I texted Megan to get her mum and dad on Skype immediately. I got a large sherry and sat and waited for them to appear—at last I could tell them the news.

They were so excited. I reminded Megan that she had bought me the painting. I don't think she remembered but Emma did. I told them about Roy taking it to college and the fire, the long wait to the auction, going to London in the car. About the mop and bucket painting that went for £28,000 and the amount of money spent in thirty minutes. I'm not sure if they were fascinated or stunned. Megan said it was like a fairy tale and she was delighted that it was all her doing and I promised her a special present when I got to Australia. I never stopped talking and Emma cried all the way through the conversation she was so pleased. The baby was due in December so it was an extra special time. Alan went into man mode, talking about getting time off work, decorating the spare room, making an area in the garden for me to grow so I wouldn't miss my allotment. When the conversation was coming to an end, he said, 'Thank God Roy took the picture out of the shed before it was burned down or this conversation would never have happened!' I owed a lot to Roy and his keen eye. We agreed I would book a flight for the end of November with an open return ticket. Once again, I felt blessed that I had the boys in my life—especially Roy.

The next day, I took my cheque to the bank and paid it in. I couldn't book the flight until it had cleared. I went into the travel agent to look at flights and maybe a stopover to break the journey up. They were very helpful and gave me all the times and dates and said to just ring when I was ready to book and they would make all the arrangements for me. I had to wait five working days for the cheque to clear, but as soon as it did

I went down to the travel agent with Visa card in hand to pay for it.

At Last

I thought the next few months would drag, but there was so
much to do: the open day to organise, the London Pride weekend outfits, and as a treat to me and Kitty and all the boys, I
booked us into a hotel in London so we could relax and enjoy
the parade.

We caught up with our plots. We never did grow carrots but
there is always next year. The Cowboys had come on to the
site and become a great success; their gate was never closed,
everyone was welcome to view the garden and the crops they
had grown. There was always good chat to be had. Col and
Jerri took a plot on site and, with the help of The Cowboys, it
didn't take long to get it into shape. I am sure John Farthing
wouldn't have liked them having it, but he wasn't in a position
to argue.

With Col's help, Shane went back into business. Col had a
contact at the local council and impressed upon them the good
works Shane had done and vouched for him. They agreed to
give him a couple of schools—enough to start him off and for
it to be worth buying a new bus.

His ex-wife also agreed that he could see his daughter just once a week to start with and see how it goes. This was hard for Shane as he had to go to his old house to pick up his daughter and be nice to the man who took his wife, daughter and business—but he did it. As he kept saying, 'this is just the beginning, let's see where we are in five years'. He had plans.

The open day was a great success: many more people turned up than last year and we made more money. I can only surmise that the plot holders kept away in the past because of John Farthing, or possibly it just seemed that way as, in the past, he had stolen most of the money.

The boys dressed as the Tiller Girls again (which wasn't hard for them) and opened the day. Shane and Wayne brought the London Palladium stage and set it up for "Beat the Clock" and all the kids had a go. The boys pranced about all afternoon and Danny brought his Caribbean band which gave the day a real party atmosphere. Wayne kept teasing Shane that Almond Eyes would turn up at any minute—they wouldn't let him forget. Life seemed so light-hearted these days.

After Col's interview on the radio, he was contacted by a television company and asked to take part in a programme about the impact of homosexuality on families. We were delighted for him, as Jez said, Col was a real star now. The show wouldn't be shown until next year and I would be back by then.

I was going in November so before I went I dug up my sweet potatoes, such as they were. They looked more like half-starved radishes—I certainly didn't have enough for a meal. Strangely I didn't mind at all. All I wanted to do was get to Australia and see my family. I had renewed my passport, bought new clothes, got the Visa, the tickets were on the mantelpiece and the case was open on the bed, ready to be packed. I had my Australian dollars and was ready to go. I just had to be patient.

It was a cold November day when I was taken to the airport in style in Col's BMW. All three insisted on coming to see me off. I promised to Skype regularly until I got back, and as I walked through security, turned to wave; they were waving and clapping and throwing kisses. I cried all the way to my seat on the plane.

Printed in Poland
by Amazon Fulfillment
Poland Sp. z o.o., Wrocław

Printed in Poland
by Amazon Fulfillment
Poland Sp. z o.o., Wrocław

58469603R00146